T0182749

To Sir, with Love

"A gleefully shameless homage to *The Shop Around the Corner* and *You've Got Mail* that sparkles like champagne fizz."
—*Publishers Weekly* (starred review)

"A first-tier purchase."
—*Library Journal* (starred review)

"Breezy dialogue and delightful characters will fully immerse readers in this dreamy and sophisticated love story. . . . A wonderfully satisfying romance."
—*BookPage* (starred review)

"A delight—as sweet and bubbly as a glass of champagne."
—Beth O'Leary, bestselling author of *The Wake-Up Call*

"Crackling with humor and sizzling with romantic tension, this charming modern fairy tale sparkles. I couldn't put it down!"
—Alexis Daria, nationally bestselling author of *A Lot Like Adiós*

"Sweet and full of humor . . . readers will be rooting for Gracie to find her Prince Charming."
—*Booklist*

"*To Sir, with Love* will have you smiling from the first swoonworthy page to the last."
—Jill Shalvis, *New York Times* bestselling author of *The Bright Spot*

"The perfect read while sipping a mai tai on the sand."
—*Cosmopolitan*

MIRANDA IN RETROGRADE

LAUREN LAYNE

G

GALLERY BOOKS

New York   London   Toronto   Sydney   New Delhi

G

Gallery Books
An Imprint of Simon & Schuster, LLC
1230 Avenue of the Americas
New York, NY 10020

First Gallery Books trade paperback edition August 2024

GALLERY BOOKS and colophon are registered trademarks of
Simon & Schuster, LLC

Simon & Schuster: Celebrating 100 Years of Publishing in 2024

For information about special discounts for bulk purchases,
please contact Simon & Schuster Special Sales at 1-866-506-1949
or business@simonandschuster.com.

The Simon & Schuster Speakers Bureau can bring authors to your
live event. For more information or to book an event, contact the
Simon & Schuster Speakers Bureau at 1-866-248-3049 or visit
our website at www.simonspeakers.com.

Interior design by Hope Herr-Cardillo

Manufactured in the United States of America

10 9 8 7 6 5 4 3 2 1

Library of Congress Cataloging-in-Publication Data
Names: Layne, Lauren, author.
Title: Miranda in retrograde / Lauren Layne.
Description: First Gallery Books trade paperback edition. | New York :
    Gallery Books, 2024.
Identifiers: LCCN 2024004844 (print) | LCCN 2024004845 (ebook) |
    ISBN 9781668047972 (trade paperback) | ISBN 9781668047989 (ebook)
Subjects: LCGFT: Romance fiction. | Humorous fiction. | Novels.
Classification: LCC PS3612.A9597 M57 2024 (print) | LCC PS3612.A9597
    (ebook) | DDC 813/.6—dc23/eng/20240205
LC record available at https://lccn.loc.gov/2024004844
LC ebook record available at https://lccn.loc.gov/2024004845

ISBN 978-1-6680-4797-2
ISBN 978-1-6680-4798-9 (ebook)

MIRANDA
IN
RETROGRADE

APRIL

When I decided at the age of nine that I wanted to be an astrophysicist, I'd thought that meant I'd study stars someday.

Not *become* one.

Now, let's be clear. I'm not a star in the Aniston, Clooney, Streep sense of the word. Nobody stops me in the streets and asks for my picture.

In nerdy terms:

If the Clooney crowd is part of the blue-white supergiants of the universe, Dr. Miranda Reed (that's me) is more of a red dwarf–level star.

In *less* nerdy terms:

It's unlikely the paparazzi will ever be jumping out from behind a bush to catch a glimpse of me carrying groceries.

I'm not a household name, by any stretch of the imagination. But among brainy social circles?

Well, let me put it this way. I may not be *People* magazine's Person of the Year, but I *have* been *Citizen* magazine's Scientist of the Year. And I was a popular fixture on 30 under 30 lists before last year's birthday put me out of contention.

I've been a contestant on *Jeopardy!* seven times, won four times, and I've even guest-hosted the game show twice. And if you've ever watched a national morning show on a super blue moon or during a meteor shower, there's a decent chance you may have seen me.

I'm proud to say that I'm often the major networks' first call when they need someone to explain something "sciencey" to their viewers.

Here's the part in this whole not-so-humble-brag where I'm supposed to say that the pseudofame is exhausting, and that I just want to be a *regular* scientist.

But actually? I *like* bringing science to the masses. I *like* making it accessible, especially to girls and women for whom the world of STEM might seem a little historically impenetrable. And most especially, I like that on days like today, being a little bit famous provides a much-needed distraction from the fact that today is *the* day.

The one that we academics spend our entire career working toward. Waiting for.

The day we get the one tiny yes/no decision that can make or break our career:

Tenure.

"Thank you *so* much, Dr. Reed," the blond undergrad student in my office says as she zooms in on the selfie we've just taken on her cell phone.

Jennifer Müller, a student from my current Astronomy 101 course with a bright, curious mind as well a propensity for showing up late to every class, squints down at her screen. "You mind if I pop a filter on this before I post it? The lighting in here's kinda blah."

"Sure. But no Photoshopping me to make my eyes bigger or my waist smaller, or whatever," I say. "I hate that crap."

"Oh my gosh, *never*. You're so naturally pretty! I wish I could get away with wearing no makeup."

I blink.

I actually *am* wearing makeup. I mean, not a ton of it. Concealer to hide the fact that my schedule doesn't allow for much sleep, brow gel to keep my thick, trademark eyebrows in place. Mascara, because, well, who doesn't look a little better with mascara?

But apparently what I thought was subtle is in fact . . . invisible.

I make a mental note to add some lipstick to the mix.

"Thanks again for the photo," Jennifer says. "I know it's kind of lame, but my dad is *such* a fan of yours. He's going to freak."

"It's my pleasure. And I bet your dad would be even more thrilled to hear that you made it to class on time one of these days." I soften the rebuke with a smile.

Jennifer winces. "Right. Totally. Sorry. I'm just *so* not a morning person. I can't believe the department stuck you with such a crappy 8 a.m. schedule when there's a waiting list for your class. You should get top pick of time slots!"

Since she's already heading out the door, I don't bother to explain that 8 a.m. *was* my pick of times, and it's *because* of the popularity of the class that I've asked the department chair for the earliest possible time. The unpopular early morning class time means that those who enroll have to really want to be there, not those who just want to see the "*Jeopardy!* professor" in person.

3

Jennifer leaves my office with a promise to be the first student in class tomorrow morning.

Before I can get back to grading the latest batch of papers on the life cycle of stars, I'm interrupted again, this time by a fellow professor.

"Like, oh my god, it's Dr. Miranda Reed!" Elijah says in a dramatic whisper before he mimes taking rapid-fire photos, paparazzi style.

He pretends to begin untucking his shirt. "Will you sign my bra?"

I roll my eyes as Elijah Singh, professor of computational physics, flops into the chair across from me. Unlike me, Elijah's class doesn't have a waiting list.

But unlike most of my other colleagues, he doesn't seem to hold this against me.

Elijah is the closest thing I have to a friend in the cutthroat world that is the Nova University Physics Department. He's also the nearest my age, which is probably why we made the foolish attempt to date back in the day. Luckily we came to the simultaneous conclusion during date three that the most explosive thing between us is our discussions about nuclear fusion processes. He's now happily married to a lovely geologist named Sadie, and he and I have settled into an easy friendship.

He points at the recently delivered white roses on my desk and gives me an expectant grin. "I'm assuming the very lavish bouquet means I can congratulate you?"

"Hold that thought," I say, blowing out a nervous breath. "I haven't heard anything yet."

I nod at the bouquet. "The flowers are from my family. They jumped the gun a little on the congratulatory thing."

4

"Well, it was a pretty safe bet on their part," Elijah says confidently. "You might be the baby of our department, but you're also the face of it. No way the board is going to risk losing their golden goose."

I nibble the inner corner of my lip, trying to ignore the sting at his words. I appreciate the vote of confidence, but it bothers me that even my closest work friend thinks I'll get tenure because of my celebrity status. That I'm a shoo-in at one of the country's top institutes of science and technology solely because I'm better than average in front of a camera and completely comfortable before a microphone. And that I'll be a boon to the department not because I'm an extraordinary scientist, but because I've stumbled into the Carl Sagan and Neil deGrasse Tyson legacy of *popularizing* science.

It chafes.

I don't *want* to become a tenured professor because I've been on talk shows.

I want to get it on the same merit as my peers, and for the same reasons. Because I'm an excellent lecturer, because my academic writing and theories are top tier, and because I'm *good* at the science stuff.

Tenure is the ultimate mark of academic approval. And becoming a full professor at a prestigious Manhattan university like Nova is the ultimate goal. At least it is for the daughter of a Harvard mathematician and an MIT particle physicist, and the sister of a Yale chemistry professor and a Boston College microbiologist.

Academia, even more than science, isn't just what we Reeds do—it's who we *are*, going back generations. I have yet to experience a single Fourth of July on which my dad hasn't told anyone who would listen that one of his ancestors taught John

Adams at Harvard in the 1750s. There's even a recurring debate at family dinners over which of us Reeds will be the next to teach a future president.

So far, my mother has come closest; a former secretary of state once sat in her classroom and, as she is not shy about sharing, barely passed.

"It can't be a good sign that they're holding off until the end of the day to notify me of their decision," I tell Elijah, unable to keep the nerves out of my voice. "Isn't that a thing? You promote someone at the start of the day, fire them at the end of it?"

He rolls his eyes. "They're not going to fire you."

I give him a look. "In this world, being denied tenured is basically the same as being fired."

"True," he admits. "At least if you're fired, people can speculate about some juicy, scandalous reason. But being denied tenure means—"

"You're just not good enough," I say, finishing his sentence.

"Right. But you." He points a finger at me. "You *are* good enough. You're practically—"

"Sorry to interrupt. Dr. Reed. You got a minute?" Both Elijah and I look toward the door where Dr. Brenda Kowalski hovers.

Well, *hovers* perhaps isn't quite the right word. It implies a sort of flighty lightness that doesn't apply at all to Brenda, despite the brilliant professor being five foot two. She may be diminutive in stature, but her intense personality creates a large, looming presence that has most of the students, and at least half the faculty, terrified of her.

I've never counted myself among the terrified half.

In fact, I *almost* count her as a friend. Not the same type of friendship I have with Elijah, but when I joined Nova University as the youngest professor in the history of the Physics Department, Dr. Kowalski took me under her wing. Admittedly, it had felt a bit like a *dragon* wing at times, but over the years, she's become a mentor and trusted confidant.

But it's also because I know her so well that my stomach knots when I see her face. It is most definitely not the expression of someone bearing good tidings.

Elijah doesn't seem to pick up on Brenda's subdued energy because he makes some inane excuse to be on his way and gives me an excited thumbs-up behind Dr. Kowalski's back before she gently shuts the door in his face.

Brenda adjusts her glasses and clears her throat.

And then I know. *I know.*

The unthinkable is happening.

Oh.

My.

God.

I don't have much experience with failure, but I can sure as hell recognize it when it's staring me in the face.

"They're denying my tenure bid," I say, my voice somewhere between a whisper and a rasp.

She nods, looking genuinely regretful. "I asked to be allowed to tell you in private, rather than the standard practice of the decision being announced in front of the entire board."

I manage a tiny nod of acknowledgment for her thoughtfulness, but it's hard to feel much more than a flicker of appreciation. Private rejection is still rejection.

And it hurts so badly I can't breathe.

Through a fog of confusion and disbelief, I'm dimly aware that Brenda is talking. Explaining. I know that I should care about the *why*. So I try to focus as she goes on and on about misplaced priorities and my public persona being a *distraction* from the department's pursuit of science. Something about me getting special permission for a sabbatical. But it all sounds like static. Unbelievable, unthinkable bullshit *static*.

"Miranda?" she says after she finishes her explanation and I say nothing. "Are you alright?"

I'm proud of myself then, because instead of giving in to the urge to cry, I merely lift an eyebrow. *What do you think, Brenda?*

She clasps her hands in front of her, and I'm slightly gratified to see that for the first time in our acquaintance, she looks uncomfortable. "It goes without saying that we hope you'll consider our offer to go on academic leave, and then come back as a lecturer. You're incredibly talented in the classroom, Miranda. That part was never in question."

I finally find my voice, and I'm relieved that it's stronger than it was a few minutes ago when I'd uttered the unimaginable *They're denying my tenure bid*.

"I appreciate that. I'll think it over."

Immediately, something deep inside me rebels at the very thought of considering their tepid offer of lecturer, much less accepting it, but I try to remind myself that good decisions are rarely made in the heat of the moment.

Brenda studies me for a minute, and then, thankfully, seems to sense that I want to be alone, because she nods and leaves, closing my door quietly behind her.

I lose track of how long I just sit, trying to sort through thoughts that refuse to be sorted.

Finally, I reach for the note tucked into the flowers from my family. I pull the card out of its tiny envelope and, using the pen the university gave me on my one-year anniversary of being a professor, scratch out the word *Congratulations*.

In its place, I write *Condolences*.

I very carefully, and precisely, tuck the card back into its spot.

And then, in a gesture that feels both petty and deeply satisfying . . .

I toss the pen in the trash.

APRIL

'm not going to say that twinkle lights and wine can fix all the world's problems, but the combination can certainly help a little.

Four days after my career imploded, I'm indulging in a beloved ritual: Friday wine-and-cheese night with my best friend and my elderly aunt. It's not an *every*-week thing, but the three of us try to get together at least once a month. I always look forward to the gatherings, but tonight I'm feeling extra grateful to be in one of my favorite spots in the world: curled up in one of my aunt's patio chairs, surrounded by the white twinkle lights that she keeps up year-round to add what she calls *dazzle* to the ivy climbing up her latticework.

Throw in the fact that my aunt lives in part of an actual castle, and it's hard not to feel like I've just been transported to someplace downright magical.

If I believed in magic, of course.

Which, as a physicist, I cannot.

Paterno Castle is nestled in Hudson Heights, right along the Hudson River on the Jersey side. Lillian's townhouse, charmingly called Cottage One (there are four in total on the southern part of the estate), is a relatively quick cab ride from my own apartment on the Nova campus.

"Okay, here we go," Daphne says as she finds whatever app she's been looking for on her phone. She places it screen-up in front of me. "When you're ready, just hit this record button and repeat word for word what exactly these morons said to you."

"Oh, sure, I'll get right on that," I mutter into my wine. "Can't wait to relive the worst moment of my life in excruciating detail."

"Well, see, I need specific details on what happened for when I cast my revenge spell," Daphne explains with a completely straight face.

I lift an eyebrow. "You still in your witchy phase?"

"Being a witch is not a phase," she explains patiently. "It's a calling."

Lillian nods solemnly in agreement, which doesn't surprise me in the least. Last October, we'd gone out to dinner and the hostess had complimented my aunt on her witch costume, to which Lillian had replied that a black cape was only a costume when worn by a child. On a grown woman it was a *statement*.

"Hold on, back up a second," Daphne says with a frown, walking her fingers backward as though reversing the conversation. "This was the worst moment of your life?"

"Um. *Yeah*," I say with feeling.

"More than the Dan breakup?"

"Absolutely." I'm not sure what it says about my romantic history that I don't even have to pause to think about it. Probably nothing good.

Daniel Dixon was my longest—and most serious—boyfriend to date. Dan is a kind and brilliant computer engineer I'd met while getting my second doctorate, and we fell into an easy, satisfying, stable relationship. He's the kind of guy who doesn't mind when you have to work late, or that you make the same slightly dry roast chicken every single Sunday. The kind who always says thank you when you hand him a Tupperware on Monday with leftovers, just like you did last Monday, and the Monday before that.

In other words, Daniel and I had an understanding that fiery passion was overrated compared to quiet compatibility. In fact, we were *so* compatible that our last Christmas together, we'd gone ring shopping. We hadn't found the one. Which was good.

Because it turns out Daniel hadn't been *the* one.

Just before New Year's that same year, he'd been offered a job at Google's corporate headquarters in Mountain View, California.

A job offer he'd accepted without so much as a word to me.

That part had hurt. Daniel may not have set my insides aflutter, but I'd thought we were partners. And partners do not make decisions that take them across the country without telling the other person.

By February, Daniel had moved out of our place with, get this: *a handshake.*

And you know what? It had been fine. *I'd* been fine. I'd spent Valentine's Day with Daphne the way I always did, not missing Daniel in the least. We'd had fudge sundaes with good ice cream, the kind that costs like ten bucks for a tiny carton, and we'd gotten two cartons. We'd followed up the ice cream with lobster rolls, because you know what? A single grown-ass woman can eat in whatever order she wants to while watching *Thor.*

(Generally speaking, I'm not much of a movie buff. And definitely not a superhero person. But even I had a hard time resisting a film in which Natalie Portman plays an astrophysicist.)

The point is, Daniel's cool dismissal of our relationship dented my heart a little, but compared to this?

My entire career being upended?

That was nothing, and I tell my aunt and best friend as much after my aunt goes to retrieve the cheese plate from inside.

"Well, that's because that Daniel wasn't right for you," Aunt Lillian says, rejoining us on the patio and setting a more-lavish-than-usual charcuterie board in the center of the table.

"What time does the entire neighborhood arrive?" I say, gesturing at the overflowing platter.

She pats my knee as she sits beside me and lights her cigarillo. "Still just us girls. I call this comfort cheese. Making your way through a variety of cheese types can help speed up the stages of grief. At least it did for me when I lost Harold."

"For example," she continues, gesturing at a soft cheese in the corner. "Still in denial? Try this nice triple crème."

"Nope, I'm solidly in the anger phase," I say, though I scoop some of the triple crème onto a cracker anyway.

"As you should be. Icing you out because you shined more brightly than them." My aunt sniffs in disdain.

"Well, they didn't phrase it *quite* like that," I say, smiling in thanks at Daphne as she tops off my sauvignon blanc.

"How *did* they phrase it?" Daphne asks, trying to subtly hit the record button on her phone again. Apparently she's very committed to her revenge spell.

"Well." I swallow my cheese and crackers. "I was mostly in shock, so I only caught the highlights, but the general gist is that my 'fixation on science pop culture'—their words—isn't in alignment with the university's or department's goals."

"I didn't realize science pop culture was a thing," Lillian muses.

"It's *not*!" I say with feeling. "And they seem to have forgotten that it was the *university* that urged me to accept all those TV spots on *Good Morning America*, and it was the head of the tenure board himself who opted to put that picture of me hosting *Jeopardy!* on the Physics Department website. Only to decide now that all of that 'distracts from the sanctity of science.'"

I add air quotes to signal my disgust.

Daphne makes an angry hissing sound. "So, to translate it to nonbullshit terms: you're a hot wunderkind, and they can't handle being in your shadow."

Lillian nods and points her cigarillo at Daphne. "*Exactly.*" Then she frowns at her empty glass. "Would one of you be a doll and get me a fresh bottle of sherry? This one seems to have evaporated."

"I'm on it," Daphne says, standing. "Miranda, you need anything while I'm inside?"

"Tenure?" I ask hopefully.

"More wine, coming up," she says with a cheeky grin before heading across the small patio toward Lillian's home.

It's cool for April, but the three of us prefer our Friday hangouts alfresco as often as we possibly can. But since the sun is setting, I pull my aunt's blanket from the back of her chair and tuck it around her legs.

As I'm leaning over her, my aunt cups my cheeks, her chunky, assorted rings pressing pleasantly against my face. "I'm sorry, dear," she says, a wistful expression on her face. "Knowing their reasons are bullshit doesn't make it any easier."

"It's fine," I say, even though it's far from fine. "Being here helps. I always feel . . . peaceful in this place."

She gestures toward her small garden area. "It's the little fairies. They keep the aphids off my rosebushes and they sprinkle good vibes."

"Do the fairies wear red?" I ask, taking a sip of my wine.

"Some of them," Lillian says in all seriousness.

"Those aren't fairies. They're Coccinellidae."

"Sweetie, just say ladybugs," Daphne chimes in, coming back with a bottle of sherry in one hand and a bottle of white wine in the other.

She's reapplied her trademark orange-red lipstick, though as always, it looks just imperfectly perfectly mussed. That's Daphne's whole thing; her dark blond hair is always just a little tousled, her bangs just a tad too long. Her style is a compelling assemblance. She's cool French-girl chic, beachy surfer girl, and mischievous witch rolled into one tall, skinny package. She looks like she could steal your man, become your best friend, and cast a spell all in the same day.

Of course, Daphne would never steal anyone's man.

But the best friend part? Absolutely.

And maybe the witchy part, too.

Lillian calls Daphne and me the odd couple, and it's an apt title. By comparison, I'm shorter, quieter, almost always dress in slim-fitted black turtlenecks, and have exactly one persona, one facet to my personality:

Brainy.

One does not look at Dr. Miranda Reed and think, "Gosh, now there's a multifaceted woman with an air of mystery!"

16

They think, "Now there's someone who could help my daughter with her calculus homework."

Now, don't get me wrong, I love being a scientist. I love *science*. But I'll confess there are times when I envy how well rounded Daphne seems to be. And there are days when I stand in front of a classroom explaining the indisputable fact that one day, billions of years from now, our sun will die, our solar system will cease to exist, and I wonder if *I'm* missing something.

Or worse, I'll wonder if I'm doing my students a disfavor by distilling our incredible universe into a pile of facts.

Maybe that's why I'm "fixated on science pop culture," as the tenure board believes. Perhaps it's my attempt to infuse some meaning into it all, even if I'm still struggling to figure out that meaning myself.

"Lady*birds*," Lillian says, apparently still thinking about her red garden fairies as she snaps her gnarled fingers in recollection. "*That's* what he called them."

"That's what who called what?" Daphne asks, because my aunt's conversational trails can be difficult to follow even *before* she starts in on her sherry.

"My darling Harold. He was from England originally, and he always called ladybugs lady*birds*."

"*See?*" I gesture to my aunt as I turn to Daphne in triumph. "This is one of the reasons I use the scientific name."

Daf props her chin on her hand and gazes at me. "Possibly also one of the reasons you're still single, babe."

Lillian lets out a small snort, and I give them each a mock glare.

"Okay, sorry," Daphne says. "Let's get back down to business."

"What business?" I ask. "The cheese?"

17

"That," Lillian says. "And figuring out our next steps."

I smile at her choice of "we" and "our." Rationally, I know there's not much my very non-science-minded aunt can do to help me navigate a perilous career crossroads, but it's *because* she's so far out of the world of academia that her support means so much.

To say that Lillian is the black sheep of the Reed family would be like saying the sun is hot. She's my father's older sister, and a self-proclaimed black sheep. I'm *still* not quite sure I have the full story of her life, but the version she likes to tell is that she escaped her family's stifling "Bostonian clutches" to visit Manhattan when she was in her twenties. She met a wealthy New Yorker—the aforementioned *darling Harold*—and married him within a week.

He'd passed away suddenly just before I was born, but the free-spirited Lillian opted to stay here in the Cottage rather than return to the uptight Reeds in New England.

"Yeah, what happens next?" Daphne asks. "Or is it too soon to tackle that?"

"Honestly, I don't have a ton of choices," I say, lifting my shoulder.

"You can't fight it? There's no appeals process?" Daphne asks.

"Technically, there is. But it's notorious for being a bit of a joke. They *never* change their minds. And if I were rejected a second time?"—I gesture with a cracker at the board—"I'd need *a lot* more cheese."

"So are you . . . were you, like . . ." Lillian and Daphne exchange a concerned look, neither wanting to say it.

"Fired?" I say. "No. It's more like . . . getting denied for a promotion. You simply go back to the job you had. Only, the difference in my world is that the decision is final. Once you're off tenure track, you're off for good. I can still be a lecturer at Nova University. They still *want* me to be a lecturer at Nova. Just without the job security or prestige."

"Well, that's a hot pile of bullshit," Lillian declares.

"Agreed. Can't you get tenure at a different school?"

"Technically, yes," I say hesitantly. "But in reality? No school I'd want to work at will consider me for tenure once word of my rejection gets out."

"Maybe your parents could—"

"No, no," Lillian says, holding up a hand when she sees me suck in a breath. "No calling in favors with the stuffy, erudite side of the family."

I can't bear to tell my aunt that even if I wanted to ask a favor, I haven't had the opportunity. My parents and brothers have been painfully silent since I texted them the news four days ago. I wasn't expecting them to rush to the city to make me cookies or anything; we're not that kind of family. We don't do warm and fuzzy; we do facts and move on.

Case in point: for my birthday last year, they got me a collective gift of a Waterpik because I made the mistake of confessing I'd gotten my first cavity.

We're *that* kind of family.

Still, I'd have thought I'd have gotten a little something. A token "that sucks" would have sufficed.

But in their defense, this is totally uncharted water for us Reeds, *especially* for me. Since third grade, when my teacher suggested skipping me forward a year, I haven't been just a part of the high-achieving Reed family: I've been the star of it. The only girl, the youngest, the smartest . . .

Daphne reaches over and takes my hand. "You okay?"

No. I force a smile. "Yeah. And there's a little good news to come out of all this. My mentor managed to get me approved for a sabbatical for a year, if I want it."

"Do you want it?" Daphne asks. "A year off would be pretty great, right?"

A nod is all I can manage, because I'm pretty sure the sabbatical had been less for my own good, and more because the department wants to get me out of the limelight for a while.

"I say you do it. Take the year," Lillian says, tapping her cigarillo. "And do it big, honey. Travel. Take dancing lessons. Get highlights. You need money? I have lots."

"No, I'm good financially," I reassure her.

Not wealthy. But good. Comfortable. I've had very affordable on-campus housing for the past several years, which keeps costs down, plus the extra money I've made here and there from TV and lecture appearances.

"So what's the hesitation?"

"I don't . . ." I pause. "Honestly, I don't know what'd I'd *do* with a year off, even if it's just a nine-month academic year. I'd have no one to teach. Nothing to study. No access to labs."

"*Eat, Pray, Love*," Daphne says, tapping the table excitedly. "*That's* what you'd do."

"Well. Yeah. I could do those things . . ."

"No, no. I'm not talking about the verbs, I'm talking about the *vibe*. You know. *Eat, Pray, Love*."

I tilt my head in confusion at the reference. "The book about the woman who goes to Italy and wherever else to find herself?"

"Oh, *yes*," Aunt Lillian says enthusiastically around a bite of Gouda, holding up her glass for more sherry, which Daphne refills. "I loved the movie."

"I'm sure it's great," I say, "but the idea of traveling for a year doesn't really call to me."

"It's not about the travel, it's about the *emotional* journey," Daphne declares. "It's about fighting back when your life goes to shit and inventing a new life, with new rules."

"My life hasn't gone to shit." I frown, scooping up a very serious chunk of the triple crème.

Lillian points at my hand. "Note that you picked up the denial cheese when you said that."

"Well, which one is acceptance cheese?" I ask patiently. "Let's move on to that one."

"You can't *force* acceptance, you have to sort of . . . float into it," Daphne says.

I snort. "I've never floated in my life."

"Maybe that's the problem, dear," Aunt Lillian says, swiping at some fig jam on her chin. "You've only ever done things a certain way, thought about things a certain way, experienced things a certain way."

"Okay, you're not wrong," I admit slowly, since it mirrors my own thoughts lately of feeling like I'm missing a vital piece of myself, a crucial part of the human experience. "But I don't think chowing down on spaghetti is going to fix that."

"Never underestimate the power of carbs," Daphne says. "But that's not actually what I had in mind. Can I show you something?"

To my surprise, it's not a rhetorical question. She sits and waits patiently for my answer, which is a bit un-Daphne-like.

It tells me that whatever idea she has, she's very serious about it. And it has me reluctantly intrigued, so I nod.

"Okay," Daphne says, picking up her phone. "Remember how the only thing I wanted for my birthday a couple years ago was your birth date and time so I could read your natal chart? I wanted the practice?"

I manage to refrain from rolling my eyes. "I remember."
That was when Daphne had been at the height of her astrology phase, before she moved into her crystals phase (the witchy phase is relatively new).

"Okay, so you still remember your sun sign, your moon sign, and your ascendant sign?"

"Am I supposed to know what that means?" I ask warily.

"We'll get to the Big Three later," Daphne says excitedly. "For now, just read this. Just the first sentence."

She hands me her phone, and I pick it up, reading aloud for Aunt Lillian's benefit. "'A dramatic curveball is headed your way today, the kind that will destroy something you thought you wanted and send you careening, perhaps wildly, in a new direction.'"

I look up. "What is this?"

"Zodiac Zone."

I shake my head, not following.

"It's a horoscope app. You just read yours." Daphne pauses dramatically. "From *Monday.*"

I look back at her phone. "The day . . ."

"The day that a dramatic curveball took away something you thought you wanted?" Lillian says gently.

I narrow my eyes. "Not *thought* I wanted. I did want tenure. I still do."

My aunt and best friend exchange a glance that I don't like one bit, mostly because I have no idea what it means, and I loathe things I can't understand.

"Hold on, one more," Daphne says, taking her phone back, flicking her finger on the screen before handing it back. "Now read this sentence."

I sigh but once again, I read aloud. "'Today's celestial alignment suggests a dramatic and surprise shift in your romantic sphere. Embrace the change with grace and confidence, and trust this person was meant to be released from your life.'"

"*That* is from the day Daniel told you he accepted that Google job," Daphne says.

"Okay," I say slowly. "I get it. A fun coincidence. But you can't tell me that *every* Virgo was fired and dumped on those precise days. Whoever writes those things is bound to get lucky once in a while. It's called statistics, not fate."

My aunt squints at the cheese board and then cuts off a generous chunk of something blue and funky-looking.

"What's this?" I ask, giving it a sniff.

"Stilton. The bargaining cheese."

I narrow my eyes. "What is it that you think I'm bargaining?"

My aunt only smiles and takes a good, long pull on her cigarillo.

Daphne gives me a reassuring smile. "All I'm suggesting is that maybe you take this sabbatical to explore a brand-new field of study."

"Astrology," I say, unable to keep the thick layer of derisive skepticism out of my voice. "You want me to take a year, of reading my horoscope and . . . what exactly?"

"Not just reading your horoscope," Daphne says, practically bouncing with excitement. "Living by its prescriptions. It tells you to go dancing, you go dancing. It tells you to flirt with a handsome stranger, you buy the hot guy at Starbucks his latte. Stuff like that."

I hand back Daphne's phone, not wanting to admit that I feel the tiniest bit unnerved at the horoscopes' accuracy.

"But what would be my hypothesis?" I say, looking between

her and Lillian. "Even if I went with a *null* hypothesis, there's no empirical data to work with. The very nature of astrology is that it's completely subjective. So what would be the point?"

"I think the point, my dear girl"—Aunt Lillian pats my hand fondly—"is that life isn't meant to be hypothesized."

I frown, not liking that one bit. "What's life meant for, then?"

Aunt Lillian smiles. "To be *lived*."

AUGUST

My aunt's inspiring speech aside, I had no intention of signing on for Daphne's "follow my horoscope for a year" nonsense, though I did eventually decide to do the sabbatical, albeit with a compromise: I'd take the standard academic year off, but only after I finished the summer courses I'd committed to. Students had already filled the roster for those well ahead of my tenure rejection. I hadn't wanted to punish them for my failure.

So today, two months into the summer session, I'd start the same way I have every workday this summer: waiting in line for my vanilla latte between classes.

But in the near future?

I'll have a lot of time on my hands.

In the meantime?

I read my horoscope as I wait for my coffee.

Not because I'm going to turn it into a yearlong soul journey or anything.

And yet, a full four months after my conversation with Lillian and Daphne, I've found myself opening the Zodiac Zone app Daphne had suggested. Out of curiosity, and *only* curiosity, mind you.

I have to admit: the more often I read it, the more I understand it. Not *believe* it. But I find a certain comfort in feeling like there are some things planned for the day that are way out of my control.

And that all I have to do is follow some instructions on how to navigate my horoscope.

Thanks to Daphne and Google, I've learned the proper way to read one's horoscope is by looking at your *ascendant* sign, also known as the rising sign. It's the constellation that was rising on the eastern horizon at the exact time of your birth. For me, that's Gemini.

If I may put on my scientist hat here for a moment? This sounds a bit like nonsense to me because it's so very *earth* centric. It's a big-ass universe out there, but astrologists would have us believe that our very destiny and personality is determined by what was happening on the eastern horizon on a single planet the moment we were born?

Still, I've since learned that the horoscope predictions Daphne had me read that night at Lillian's house were in fact my *rising* sign horoscope. And it was more eerily accurate than I'd like to admit.

Even to myself.

Because here's the thing with me and astrology. As a scientist, not only have I been trained to think such things are nonsense, I've *preached* it. I open the first day of every semester in *all* of my classes with a call for any and all questions. I make a point to clarify that none are too silly or far-fetched. And as a result, I have never had a single intro to astronomy or cosmos course in which someone hasn't gathered the courage to ask—usually hopefully—if astrology is real.

To which I have without hesitation asserted:

No. Absolutely not.

I try to soften the blow to the hopeful student as best I can, explaining that thousands of years ago, astrology was absolutely understandable. Early humans would try to make sense of the world around them by what they could see and observe: the constellations and planets in our own solar system.

But we know so much more now. We know that our solar system is one of *thousands* in a galaxy that is one of hundreds of billions of galaxies. And that's just in the observable universe.

So, does *any* part of me think that the location of the constellations and planets at the day and time of my birth have any bearing on the events of my life?

I just can't believe that. I just *can't*.

But sometimes? I want to. I want to be like Daphne, who believes not just in astrology, but in *all* the stuff. Numerology. Astral projection. The power of crystals.

And if you're wondering how someone who believes in vortexes became best friends with someone who reads the *Journal of Applied Physics* . . . me, too.

But according to Daphne, our meeting was simply part of the universe's master plan. We were twenty when we met. I'd been in the midst of getting my first doctorate, and Daphne had been putting herself through design school by waitressing at my favorite café studying spot. Somewhere between her slipping me free pieces of apple pie she knew I couldn't resist and me giving input on her latest project, we'd just sort of felt meant for each other, in a sisterly kind of way. As though we each existed to plug a hole in the other person's life.

Because I'd skipped ahead several years in school and had begun my undergrad at sixteen instead of the usual eighteen, I'd always been younger than my classmates, and thus didn't have any solid, lasting friendships. Daphne's closest childhood friend had recently relocated to Seattle, and as she'd put it, she missed having "a loved one's life to meddle with."

So she'd begun to meddle with mine. And even though this has meant that I now know way more about angel numbers and tarot than I ever thought possible, I wouldn't have it any other way.

So here I am. Pulling up my horoscope.

Just for fun.

In matters of the heart, keep your senses sharp today, darling Gemini. A chance meeting with a charming stranger could lead to a romantic encounter beyond your wildest dreams. This person may seem like a knight in shining armor, ready to swoop in and save the day, even as they nudge your life in a new direction.

"Fantastic," I mutter, slipping my phone back into my bag. "I'll be sure and secure a wedding venue right away."

"Morning, Dr. Reed," says Eric, the smiling barista whose shift always aligns with my schedule. "Usual?"

"Please," I say as I pay with my Starbucks app and add a tip.

Eric glances over his shoulder toward his fellow employees, then leans forward. "How about a cake pop? On the house."

I blink. "Oh. Well. Sure. Do I look depressed or some-thing?"

He grins. "Nah. Just sort of felt like offering."

"Well, thanks. I feel like accepting."

I'm taking the free treat when something occurs to me. "Hey, would you call this a knight-in-shining-armor situation?"

He tilts his head. "Sorry?"

"Nothing, never mind." I shake my head.

Eric is handsome, in a cute-but-*way*-too-young-for-me kind of way. He's also not a stranger.

Sorry, horoscope. I tried.

A couple of minutes later, I walk out of Starbucks with latte in hand. It's started to rain, which I hadn't counted on. I don't have an umbrella or a hood, but I do have good cross-walk luck, and am able to cross Lafayette without having to stand in the rain. And as I approach Broadway, the light is again in my favor.

I'm just stepping into the crosswalk when I hear the blare of a car horn from way too close, and I turn my head to see a taxi barreling through a red light without slowing down. It's hurtling toward me faster than I can move, but the same sec-ond I realize I'm about to get hit, I'm pulled backward with so much force my latte splatters to the ground.

"Hey! What an *asshole*!" a pedestrian yells.

I'm inclined to agree, but my heart's beating too hard at the near catastrophe.

"You okay?" a male voice asks from directly behind me.

I turn toward him and realize two things at once: he must have been the one to pull me out of harm's way, and he's . . . perfect.

I've always liked to say that I don't have a type, but I've

been horribly wrong about that, or maybe I simply had to see my type to recognize it.

You know that strange sense you have when someone seems just made for you? Like they were created to check all your boxes?

This is him.

Tall without towering, strong without being brawny. His blue eyes are friendly, his face handsome if not quite symmetrical. His hair is not quite blond, but not brown, either. His smile is *perfect* and crooked and just a tiny bit shy.

And maybe it's just wishful thinking, but I swear he's looking at me with that same dazed *it's you* that I'm feeling right now.

Just to be safe, I sneak a peek at his left finger, and my heart leaps to find it bare.

When my eyes return to his face, his gaze takes just a moment to snap back to mine, and somehow I just know that he's done the same analysis of my left hand.

"You okay?" he asks again, dipping just slightly to bring his eyes more level with mine, as though needing to reassure himself.

"Yeah! Yep. Good. Very good. Yep."

So eloquent, Miranda.

I've never been particularly adept at flirting, but usually I can hold my own in conversation and manage sentences longer than two words.

"Thank you," I say, trying to sound more normal. "For . . . well, obvious reasons." I wave at the intersection.

He shakes his head, disgusted. "It's a miracle nobody was hurt. He could have killed someone."

"Thankfully the only casualty was one tall, triple-shot vanilla oat milk latte," I say as I bend down to pick up my now-empty cup and throw it away in a nearby trash can.

"I . . ." He hesitates. "Can I buy you another one?"

My heart leaps in joy, then sinks to my feet when I realize that I don't have time for a second trip to Starbucks. "I wish. But I have a class starting in just a couple minutes that I'm likely to be late to."

"Ah. Grad student?"

"Professor. Physics. Astronomy, specifically," I blurt out.

"Oh. You're kidding." He lets out a startled laugh. "My daughter is completely obsessed with anything related to the night sky."

Daughter.

Woof.

I mean, not that I don't love kids, but a *daughter* obviously has a *mother*, which means . . .

I smile, trying to keep the disappointment off my face.

"I don't suppose you do private tutoring?" he asks with a grin. "It would kill my ex to know I found Kylee an astronomy tutor before she did."

Devastation makes a sharp reversal back to delight.

"I don't currently," I admit. "But I've always wanted to."

So, this is a blatant lie. I have never in my life thought about private tutoring. But as far as lies go, this one isn't going to keep me up at night, because I'm also not *opposed* to tutoring.

Especially daughters of really cute single dads.

"Amazing," he says, reaching into the pocket of his suit. "Here's my card. If you're not just being polite because I very dashingly saved you from a horrible death, text me. Email. Call."

I accept the card, obviously. Christian Hughes.

"'CFO of OmniLogic Solutions,'" I read aloud. The company name seems vaguely familiar—they make computer chips, or some something like that. "Impressive."

"Impressive enough to get your name?" he asks hopefully. Charmingly.

"Dr. Miranda Reed," I say, extending a hand.

His palm closes over mine, warm and strong and perfect.

"It was really nice to meet you, Miranda. I would love to repeat it. Minus the whole near-death element."

"I'd like that, too."

He smiles and winks. "Then I'll hear from you. I hope."

I stare at him for a moment too long after he walks away, before jolting a little as I realize the time. I run the rest of the way to the Physics Department building, but even still, I'm late for class for the first time in years.

And the first time *ever*, my heart's not in the lecture.

I've spent my entire life blindly, diligently obeying the laws of physics, the rules of nature, the strict prescriptions of scientific study.

And yet, today I find that my attention isn't on science at all.

It's about my horoscope's prediction of a charming stranger. A knight in shining armor who saves the day.

And sends me in a new direction.

I've finally figured out what that new direction's going to be.

The summer session is nearly over, and then it's time to break all the rules. To reinvent myself.

To become someone other than Dr. Miranda Reed, scientist.

I'm going to take Daphne's advice and *Eat, Pray, Love* by way of astrology.

I'm going to take my aunt's suggestion.

I'm going to *live*.

SEPTEMBER

You *promise* you're not leaving because of me?" I ask my aunt. "Because Daphne knows someone who's looking to sublet their studio in the Lower East Side. I don't want to run you out of your home."

Lillian applies a swipe of shockingly bright pink lipstick, then pats my cheek. "Darling girl, I love you more than anything in this world, and that includes that dear, nerdy lump that you call a father and I call a brother. But that's still not enough to compel me to stick around these parts once the weather starts to turn. I'd be heading to Palm Beach whether or not you needed a place to stay."

And I *do* need a place to stay.

The university had let me continue leasing my on-campus apartment through the summer term, but since I won't be an active lecturer this academic year, I'd had to move out.

Not that I'd *wanted* to stay. I'd stopped feeling like I belonged there the second I learned of the tenure board's decision. Everything I'd been focused on suddenly became irrelevant.

When Lillian had heard, she'd insisted I move into the

Cottage, since it coincided with her annual migration to Florida and would otherwise be empty.

"And besides"—she gives my cheek another tap before checking her lipstick in the entryway mirror—"I rather like knowing someone is here to take care of the plants."

Lillian lifts an eyebrow and meets my gaze in the reflection. "You *will* take care of the plants. And the fairies."

I can't tell if she's kidding or not about the fairies. I doubt it, so I nod, balancing the stack of paper where she's written instructions on plant care in her slanted, looping penmanship. "I've seen academic papers less detailed," I remark as I rifle through them. "I can't possibly mess this up."

"Good. And don't forget the plants on the roof. They're my favorites."

I frown. "Then why put them on the roof? I didn't even know you ever *went* to the roof."

She fluffs her hair and gives an enigmatic smile that makes me think even if she tells me, I won't understand it.

I'm guessing something to do with fairies or elves.

"I wish you didn't have to go so soon. It would have been nice to be roomies for a while."

"Sorry, darling. The grande dames live alone, and never in the cold."

I don't know anything about grand dames, but I do know seasons. "It's not even autumn yet."

"True. But Judith will be furious if I don't bear witness to her eightieth birthday extravaganza tomorrow. It's on a boat, which seems like a mistake with a bunch of senior citizens, and thus I can't miss it."

She turns back to me. "Though I confess I would rather

like to see what wild Miranda looks like. I want to hear daily updates."

"I don't know about *wild* Miranda. I haven't really started the Horoscope Project yet, but so far the craziest thing it's suggested is that I try a new cuisine."

The Horoscope Project is what I'm calling my yearlong commitment to living like an astrologist instead of a scientist.

Naming the endeavor had made it feel more real. And opting for the generic *project* instead of *hypothesis* or *experiment* felt like a gratifying middle finger to the knowledge-based world that betrayed me.

My aunt is studying me. "Have you called that boy yet?"

"He is in his thirties, Lillian. With a kid of his own."

She waggles a finger. "Don't try to distract me because you're being a chicken."

"I'm . . . waiting for the right time. I had to grade final exams and papers, I was moving, I was—" I break off.

"Making excuses? It's been almost two weeks since you called me all gooey-voiced after almost becoming roadkill."

"That's *beautiful*," I say. "I had no idea you were such a poet. And I'll call him. When my horoscope says I should."

"Oh no you don't." She shakes her head. "You're not going to use astrology the same way you did science."

"What's that supposed to mean?!"

"It means that I don't want to see you shift one set of rules for another set of rules, all so you can keep yourself safe and tidy. You'd be missing the whole point."

"Which is?" I ask, curious for her take.

Instead of answering the question, she gets a slightly wistful look on her face. "Do you remember summers when you

37

were a girl? I had that big house I rented up in the Hudson Valley, and you and your brothers would come stay with me for a couple months."

"Sure, of course. I loved those days."

"You loved those *nights*," she amends. "You spent every clear evening flat on your back in the grass, staring up at the sky. You loved it."

"Well, of course. I've wanted to be an astronomer since I was nine."

She shakes her head. "No. That's the Wikipedia version of Dr. Miranda Reed's story. And it's the story you've told yourself, no doubt fed subtly to you by your parents around the time they started sending you to summer science camp instead of my place."

"Oh, Lillian." I reach for her hand. "I'm sorry. I never realized that you must have felt—"

"Posh." She waves this away impatiently. "It has nothing to do with me. I took on *quite* the virile paramour the first summer you quit coming to visit. This is about you, darling. You don't remember, or don't want to remember, but it wasn't until you were twelve that you declared you wanted to be an astronomer. I remember because I pitched in to help with that expensive telescope for your twelfth birthday."

I frown. "I don't understand. If I was obsessed with the night sky before that . . ."

"You were obsessed, but not with cosmetic microwave background and dark matter."

"*Cosmic*," I correct. "Cosmic microwave background."

She lets out a dramatic sigh but refuses to be distracted from her point. "Don't forget who you were before you decided you wanted to add all those fancy *doctor*s to your name."

"Who was I?" I ask, genuinely curious, as Lillian heads toward the front door.

"A girl who believed that the stars were *magic*, that the moon held secrets, and who the universe had a plan for. And no," she adds, giving me a pointed look over her shoulder. "That plan wasn't tenure. You wanted to be a rock star."

A few hours after Lillian's departure, the movers arrive with my boxes. Luckily, as far as moves go, this one's not terribly overwhelming.

Since Cottage One is already furnished, I had most of my furniture put into a storage unit just down the road. Same with all of my kitchen stuff, since Lillian has all of that as well. She'd generously suggested that I could move her stuff out while I was here, to make it feel like my own place. But I realized I'm not even sure what my own place would look like. Or rather, I *do*. It would look a lot like the drab little one-bedroom on-campus apartment that I'd lived in for six years, yet somehow failed to leave a mark on of any kind.

I'd always meant to make some sort of effort to settle in. To hire a decorator, or at the very least, hit up Pinterest for some DIY inspiration. Hell, even a generic image framed on the wall would have been something. Instead, the poor space had been a house, but never a home. You would know that *someone* lived there—there was a couch, coffee table. Kitchen table, chairs, bed. But any insight about the person? The furniture had been neutral, the walls bare. Even the stacks of books, which had been everywhere, had been tucked tidily into corners, not displayed or laid out on the coffee table with any sort of pride or enthusiasm.

That had been both the hardest and the most satisfying part of the moving process. Stacking my dozens of academic books and papers into boxes, taping them up, and then banishing them along with my boring furniture to storage.

Practically speaking, it had been necessary, given that Lillian's place—and personal style—is basically the opposite of my own. Lillian likes to call herself a maximalist, which is a euphemistic way of saying she's a borderline hoarder. Every corner has a quirky lamp, funky statue, or well-loved houseplant. Every shelf is covered in gnome figurines, snow globes, or little trinkets she's collected from trips and friends over the years.

But while there'd been no physical room for my books, I realized I didn't want to make mental room for them, either. Or maybe I *did* want to, and that had made it all the more necessary to put them out of reach. If I wanted to uncover a new Miranda, a Miranda who is more than facts and intellect, I needed to make room for a new kind of knowledge. Academia has been my haven, my books my security blanket. So away they'd gone until the end of the Horoscope Project.

Which, on that note . . .

I go to the front door, where Lillian has placed my packages that arrived the day before. I guess I'll have to make room for some books after all, but not ones about quantum particles. Daphne had put together an astrology for beginners reading list for me, and I'd dutifully ordered every last one. I'm just beginning to take them out of their boxes when the phone I've shoved into the back pocket of my jeans buzzes.

I pull it out, and—I'm not proud of this—I very nearly silence the thing and put it right back into my pocket.

Instead, I take a breath, find the nearest bottle of wine, and . . .

"Hi, Mom!"

She lets out a tiny, disappointed sigh, as though I didn't quite nail my greeting. It was probably too enthusiastic.

"Miranda. I'm surprised you picked up. Isn't today moving day?"

"Why do you say that in the same tone that someone might say *D-day*?" I ask, even though I already know.

Aunt Lillian and my mom are like two magnets with the south poles facing one another. No amount of pushing will ever make them connect. And believe me, I've tried.

I get along with my mother, more or less. I get along with Lillian. Which makes me their *only* common ground.

My mother is a mathematics professor at Harvard. It sounds a little cliché, but her idea of a thrilling night off is a cup of her blueberry tea and a documentary series about code breakers. Lillian, on the other hand, carries a flask in her purse, tucked alongside a pack of cigarillos and her beloved Harlequin romance novel of the month. And she only likes "the good and smutty ones."

"I understand that your newly unemployed status leaves you essentially homeless. What I can't understand is why you'd choose to retreat to your aunt's . . . realm, rather than come home to Boston where your family can rally around you and help you get back on your feet."

"I *am* on my feet, Mom. I'm just taking a sabbatical. A perfectly normal, and encouraged, part of the academic process."

"A sabbatical is meant to reinvigorate one's academic rigor, not neglect it completely for some ancient pseudoreligion."

I'm pouring myself a nice glass of wine, and with that last statement, I give myself an extra splash.

"You talked to Jamie," I say, resigned.

I have two older brothers: Brian, a chemistry professor at Yale, and Jamie, a microbiologist at Boston College. I adore them both, but I'm a little closer to Jamie in both age and temperament. Brian is a sweetheart deep down; it's just buried beneath a thick layer of intensity and a fondness for pontificating, especially to his younger sister. Jamie is more personable, and easier to talk to. He'd been the first in my family to break the ice after hearing about my job, and in gratitude, I'd found myself confessing to him about the Horoscope Project.

I'd also asked him not to tell a soul. A request that had apparently been ignored.

"Astrology, Miranda? You yourself have been very vocal about its impossibility."

"Implausibility," I say, correcting her. "There's a difference."

After a stiff pause, she says, "Yes, dear. I am aware. My point is, we both know that celestial bodies aren't up there plotting your and my life. I realize you've had a setback, but this isn't the way—"

I interrupt. "Why didn't you call?"

There's another pause, this one surprised. "When?"

"After I texted you guys saying that I didn't get tenure. Why did nobody call? Not for *weeks*, and even when Jamie set up the group FaceTime on Father's Day."

"Well, to your point, it *was* Father's Day, dear. I hardly think your dad's ideal day involved revisiting your . . . misstep?"

I know it's coming, but it still stings. "My misstep," I repeat carefully, taking a tiny sip of wine. "You do realize that I did nothing wrong, right? Other than being more famous than my colleagues?

"And you know what?" I add, warming up to my subject. "Even if I was wrong, even if I was a colossal screwup, you're my *mom*."

"Of course I am!" To her credit, she sounds both surprised and upset that I'm upset. "What is it you needed that I didn't provide?"

I exhale, because it's one of those things where if it has to be explained, it misses the point entirely.

"I don't know, Mom," I say tiredly. "I guess I was just hoping for . . . support."

"Exactly!" Her voice lights up. "That's what we want to do, honey. It's why I think you should come home. Your dad and brothers and I can try calling in some favors. I'm sure there are some guest lecturing opportunities . . ."

My sip of wine is much bigger this time. "Mom. I appreciate that you mean well, but I don't want to be the family's sad little charity case. I'm not even sure I want to be around the collegiate world anymore."

"So you're going to just . . . be an eccentric fruitcake?"

I smile, more amused than offended, because my mother sounds more befuddled than anything else, as though she literally cannot understand what I'm trying to do here.

"Mom," I try to keep my voice gentle. "Have you ever felt a little . . . flat? Like only one part of your soul is lit up?"

"Well, science has shown us there's no such thing as a soul, dear."

Welp. I tried.

"Is this because you're still single?" she asks. "Because, you know, Brian's friend Scott is divorced now, and I think he's looking to start dating again. You always liked Scott."

I don't even think I know a Scott.

"I'll think about it," I say. "But starting tomorrow, it'll really depend."

"On what?"

I grin, a little devil on my shoulder nudging me forward, and I'm suddenly more excited about the year ahead than ever. "My horoscope."

♍ VIRGO SEASON

*Sit up a little straighter today, darling Gemini.
Your planetary ruler, Mercury, stations and turns
direct today. While this signals a shift away from the
indecisive confusion of past weeks, lingering fog will
persist, so don't make any big decisions.
In better news, today's Sun-Uranus trine will
recharge and motivate you. This is a good time to
start a home-improvement project, something you
haven't thought of previously that will
suddenly feel vital.*

A few days after Lillian's departure, I start my morning the way I have been since the start of the Horoscope Project—with a cup of coffee and the Daphne-recommended Zodiac Zone app. Apparently it's one of the few astrology apps that doesn't just ask for your birthday and spit out the "sun sign" that most people think of as their sign. This one requires your birthday, time of birth, and place of birth so it can assess your *full* natal chat, and thus give you a more accurate reading.

45

Says Daphne.

I have yet to be convinced, but one thing I can say about its daily predictions? They can be *annoying*.

I groan aloud in the empty kitchen as I read today's horoscope: home improvement? *Yuck*.

I am not exactly what you would call *handy*. Not with arts and crafts, not with hobbies, and most definitely not with home-improvement projects.

Also, because I haven't had a chance to crack open any of the astrology books amid settling into Lillian's, I don't have a clue what the heck a planetary ruler is.

Maybe I don't have to listen to it.

I pick up my phone and decide to FaceTime Daphne over breakfast.

"Hello, darling Gemini!" she says the second she picks up.

"You read my horoscope, didn't you?" I ask.

And since she's the one who recommended this particular app, I'm betting we read the exact same horoscope.

This is actually one thing that bothers me about astrology. One of the many. That there are hundreds, if not thousands, of horoscope sources out there, none of them identical, many of them not even close. How are you supposed to know which one is the best one?

The right one?

Daphne tells me it's about faith, so . . . I'm trying. I've decided to stick with just this one app for now, not letting myself get confused by any conflicting sources. Plus, the scientist in me likes the idea of a constant for this little project. The same horoscope source every single day provides that for me.

"Um, of course I read it," Daphne says, sounding affronted.

"Though I did that even before you decided to embrace your spirituality."

I wrinkle my nose.

"Too soon to throw around *spirituality*, huh?" she says with a laugh.

"Baby steps. I want to understand this thing on an intellectual level. What is a house ruler, and why is mine Mercury?" I ask before taking a bite of cereal.

"Oooh," she says, pursing her lips. "That pesky wasteland of a planet. Bet you're excited to be out of retrograde, huh? Okay, anyway. Um, planet rulers. So . . . your rising sign is Gemini, right? And Mercury rules Gemini. Ergo, your house ruler. Sort of like the captain of the ship," she continues. "Your house ruler sort of steers the whole thing."

"So I can't ignore it?"

"Not without consequence. Why, not excited by the . . . what was it? House project?"

"Do you think vacuuming counts?" I ask, brightening. "I have to do that."

"Vacuuming is a chore, not a project."

"Damn." I take another bite of cereal, frowning as I chew. "Why?"

"Why isn't vacuuming a project?"

"No, why does Mercury rule Gemini?" I say. "Who's your house ruler? As a Libra."

"Venus."

"*Why?*" I say again.

Daphne wrinkles her nose. "Okay, fine. I don't actually know how the house ruler is determined."

"Hmm, okay," I say, relenting. "I'm sure it's in one of the books I bought."

"Probably," she says, looking bemused. "Just remember the point of this whole thing is to get *away* from books for a little while."

"But I'm a Virgo sun!" I protest, knowing she'll appreciate the reference. "This is how we do things."

"Fair enough." Daphne smiles. "How's the settling-in process going?"

"Bumpy," I admit. "I slammed my finger in the car door so hard I nearly *broke* it and am now wearing a splint." I hold up the hand to show her. "And then I got that cold going around. And *then* Lillian's hot water heater broke, and the guy who came to replace it got violently sick in the bathroom. That's all I want to say about that—why are you smiling at my pain?"

"I'm not," she says with a laugh. "It's just . . . this is all *so* Mercury-retrograde stuff."

I almost open my mouth to remind her that planets can't actually move backward, and that it's merely an optical illusion caused by the planets moving at different speeds from each other, but that's scientist Miranda talking.

Astrologist Miranda is supposed to believe that Mercury rules all types of communication, and when it's in retrograde, there is all sorts of turbulence and disruption down here on Earth. Wires getting crossed, a general sense of indecision and mayhem, blah-blah-blah.

I take my empty bowl to the sink, and then let out a frustrated growl when I glance out the window.

"I've gotta run," I tell Daphne. "A chubby bunny is munching contentedly on one of Lillian's plants again."

"Oh, cute! Bunnies are my spirit animal! He must know you're talking to me."

I end the call before she can see my eye roll.

I hurry to the front door, intentionally making all sorts of noise to scare the little bringer of destruction away. The bunny is cute, I'll give him that, but he's wreaking havoc on Lillian's "babies," and I haven't had the heart to tell my aunt that there's no good place on the patio for her babies to get the right amount of sun *and* be out of reach of critters.

I'm no botanist, but I've been musing all week over a way to regulate the temperature out here and provide some sort of shelter . . .

"Oh. Okay," I murmur aloud as inspiration strikes. I need a greenhouse.

I could *build* a greenhouse. That could be my home project.

I dash back into the house and begin researching.

Several hours later, I'm surprised to find that I'm the most excited and motivated I've been in days.

Just like my horoscope said I would be.

♍ VIRGO SEASON

Apparently, even task-oriented Virgos can't build a green-house in a single day. I couldn't even *plan* one in a day, though I made a valiant effort. If I'm being really honest with myself, it chafed my ego a bit that the undertaking hadn't been as effortless as I expected.

The thing is . . . I'm kind of, sort of *technically* a genius, says the IQ test my parents put us kids through the same way other parents sign their children up for soccer camp. It's not something I talk about a lot, or even think about often, but the reality is that most things come fairly easy to me.

Apparently household projects are out of my wheelhouse, because even though I spent the whole day online researching how to go build a greenhouse, I don't feel like I made much progress.

It's not until I'm getting ready for bed that evening that I realize I spent so much time focusing on the *downstairs* plants that I forgot about Lillian's precious rooftop flowers.

Setting my Waterpik aside, I stick my feet into fuzzy slippers and pull on a sweater that's so cozy and oversized it hangs below the hem of my pajama shorts. Then, after I fill the watering can, I make my way up the skinny, winding staircase to the roof.

While I'm still a little puzzled by my aunt's insistence on this rooftop chore, I don't actually mind it. In fact, it's quickly become my favorite part of my routine. Not so much for the mundane plant-watering task itself, which takes just a few moments. It's more that the task takes me to the roof, which takes me to the *stars*.

Even more painful to admit than the fact that I can't build a greenhouse is the realization that despite having built an entire career around studying the cosmos, I can't remember the last time I actually *looked up.* Or when I last appreciated the night sky for its beauty, and not its educational value.

It's during these quiet late-night moments up on Lillian's roof—even more so than when reading my horoscope every morning—that I sense *another* Miranda. A Miranda who allows herself to see stars as twinkling little diamonds meant for making wishes, and not the giant spheres of plasma that Dr. Miranda Reed knows them to be.

Technically speaking, it's mediocre stargazing. Lillian's house is too close to the light pollution from Manhattan to see things properly.

But the time feels sacred and special all the same.

I realize halfway up the stairs that I won't be doing even mediocre stargazing tonight. I've already taken out my contacts and neglected to grab the glasses I wear in the evening and early morning.

Still, since it's not like I need twenty-twenty vision to dribble some water onto flowers, I don't bother to go back down to grab them.

"Hi, darlings," I murmur to the plants, sticking my finger

into the soil. Lillian's extensive written instructions for her plants talk a lot about poking the dirt to test it. At first, this had made zero sense to me, but as I automatically stick my pointer finger into the cool, moist soil, I'm pleased to realize I think I'm finally getting a feel for being a plant mom. I could tell they hadn't needed *any* water after a late summer thunderstorm yesterday, and I can tell now they only need a little sip.

Lillian refers to the pretty purple flowers as her "Buzzes," which I thought had just been Lillian being Lillian, but have since learned is actually a thing. Buzzes are a variety of a flowering shrub called buddleia. They bloom right up to the first frost, and then I can ease back on the watering. I'd been annoyed by this at first, but now I'm sad I only have another month or so to enjoy them. They're also known as the "butterfly bush," and I make a mental note to come up during the day sometime in the next few weeks to catch sight of the butterflies their fragrance is supposed to attract.

"Good evening, Lillian's niece."

I squeak and drop the watering can, pivoting toward the unexpected slow rumble of a masculine voice.

Thanks to the lack of light and my currently uncorrected nearsightedness, I can't make out much detail, but there is definitely a *man* on the neighboring roof not ten feet away from my own.

"Is that an easel?" I ask, blinking at the stand in front of him.

"Lillian did say you were a genius. A real marvel to see it in action," he says in a sardonic, indifferent tone.

I blink, a little taken aback by the unfounded rudeness.

"I just mean . . . how can you even see—forget it." If this

strange man on the roof isn't going to bother with small talk, then neither will I. "How did you know who I was?" I add with narrowed eyes.

"Lillian emailed all the neighbors. Let us know you'd be living here while she was gone."

"Interesting. She didn't mention *you*."

He shrugs and picks up what looks like black chalk—charcoal? Is that a thing artists use?—and because it's so quiet up here, I can hear the scratch of it over the canvas as he resumes his work.

I pick up the watering can, which thankfully still has just enough water to satisfy the Buzzes' needs, but instead of finishing up with my plant duties, I continue to glare at Lillian's neighbor.

"So. That was an opening for you to introduce yourself," I say after a long silence.

There's no pause in the scratching sound of the charcoal on canvas, and he doesn't bother turning his head my way when he responds. "Archer."

"Archer. Is that a first name? Last name?"

He glances over, and though I can't make out much of anything about his features in the dark, I can see a blink-and-you'll-miss-it flash of white in the moonlight. "Why? You going to cross-reference my story with Lillian? Make sure I'm not some creepy squatter who lives on the roof?"

I scratch my nose, because that's actually exactly what I'd been planning to do.

"Last name," he says, smile gone, bored again. "And don't worry, Lillian's niece. Your aunt knows me. What are you doing up here?"

"Watering her favorite plants," I say, gesturing with the

watering can toward the Buzzes. "Lillian likes the rooftop ones watered at night."

That seems to get his attention. He glances briefly to the plants in question. "I come up here almost every night it's not raining, and I have *never* seen those plants in my life." He points with his charcoal.

I blink in surprise. "What?"

"For that matter, I've never seen Lillian up here, either."

Now I'm genuinely perplexed, because he doesn't *seem* like he's lying, but Lillian's instructions had been very precise. "Are you sure?"

He shrugs.

I frown down at the plants. "I wonder why she moved them up here. A seasonal thing, maybe?"

He doesn't reply, and I realize he's gone back to his work once again, as though I'm not even here. It's hardly an ego booster, but then I'm not the femme fatale type. This is hardly my first time being disregarded by a man, so I don't take much offense.

Curious about Archer in spite of his overt rudeness, I walk to the edge of my rooftop toward his. It's not a large space. In fact, there's not even a foot-wide gap between our buildings. Enough to lose a set of keys forever, but not enough for anyone to risk falling between them.

The footprint of Archer's rooftop is about the same as mine. Now that I think about it, I do vaguely remember noticing the rusted chair before.

But the easel is new, as is the stool beside it. The man is *definitely* new, and I'm *not* enjoying the development.

I hadn't really realized it until I'd spotted the unexpected company, but I've come to think of the roof as *my* space. The rest of the home still very much feels like Lillian's. But up here, with the view of the stars and the Manhattan skyline? This is Miranda's.

And now I have to share it. I don't like that in the least.

"How can you draw at night if you can't see what you're doing?" I say, finally giving in to my curiosity.

"It's not like I'm out here in a thunderstorm with a waxing crescent." He nods slightly upward. "It's clear. Waxing gibbous."

I cross my arms, peevishly annoyed that he knows this. "You know your moon phases."

"You would, too, if you liked to draw by moonlight."

"Are you a professional artist?"

His attention refocuses on his canvas. "Yes, I make money from my painting."

"That's not what I asked."

"Isn't it?"

I consider this. "Yes, I suppose it was."

I sense rather than see his eyes flick briefly my way, perhaps surprised at the admission, before returning to his work. "Not *this* work," he says, nodding at the canvas in front of him. "I sell the stuff I create in my studio. This is just for me."

"Can I see?" I ask curiously.

"Was 'just for me' not clear?"

"You're not very friendly."

Instead of acknowledging this, he lifts a glass off the stool and takes a sip of whatever's in it as he studies me. "What's your name, Lillian's niece? It was probably in the email, but I forget."

"Dr. Miranda Reed, PhD."

He lets out a quick laugh and sets the glass back down. "You always introduce yourself like that?"

I frown. "Usually. I don't want people to think I'm a medical doctor. If there's an emergency, I won't be much use."

He simply shakes his head and goes back to his work.

I narrow my eyes. "You said you come up here every night the moonlight is good, but that isn't true. There was a full moon in Pisces on August 30, and you were not up here."

"A full moon in Pisces? Randy, what is it with you and extraneous information?"

"Randy?" I repeat.

"Well, I'm not calling you Dr. Miranda Reed, PhD," he says with a rather spot-on impression of my "teacher voice," which sometimes finds its way out of the classroom.

"I was not up here on the full moon in Pisces," he says, "because I've been out of town the better part of a month."

"Oh. Do you travel often?"

"Is that hope I hear in your voice?"

"Well." I cross my arms. "We aren't exactly hitting it off, are we? And if I'm up here every night, and you're up here most nights . . ." I trail off, because my implication is clear.

"I see. I, too, enjoy my solitude. How about a schedule?"

"Sure!" I say, pleased and surprised by his agreeability.

He nods. "Great. I'll come up here every night the weather and moon permit, and you . . . never."

I make an exasperated noise, but instead of relenting, he shrugs. "Let's not forget, Dr. Miranda Reed, PhD, I've lived here the better part of four years, and *you* long enough to cite only one full moon. In Pisces."

With a resigned sigh, I return to the Buzzes to give them the last few drops from the watering can. "I see I took on the wrong home project."

"What are you muttering about, Randy?"

"I thought I was meant to build a greenhouse downstairs," I explain. "But I don't think that should be my first home-improvement endeavor."

"No?" His indifferent tone and the fact that he's gone back to his work don't invite conversation, but I decide to tell him anyway.

"I'm thinking I should build a fence. Taller than a fence. A barrier," I say when he doesn't acknowledge me.

"On the *roof*," I say a little louder.

"Randy," he says. Finally, something surpasses the boredom: exasperation. "Do you always talk this much?"

"No. Not at all, actually." I pause. "Something we have in common. Only I'm much more likable about it."

He lets out something that sounds like a laugh, and I'm pretty sure he tries to bite it back, but I hear it anyway. It pleases me.

At least it does until he goes back to drawing without another word.

"I'm going back downstairs," I announce.

"So soon?"

I roll my eyes, even though he can't see it.

"Hey. Randy?" he says just as I'm about to retreat inside.

I glance across the roof and see one more flash of the smile in the moonlight. "Same time tomorrow?"

My only response is to let the door slam a little too loudly behind me.

VIRGO SEASON

Today is all about forgiveness and amendments,
dear Gemini. You'll be itching to restore harmony,
so take the first step by mending fences with
someone you've had a recent conflict with,
perhaps by undertaking a shared goal.
Their role in your life is not what it first seemed . . .

Listen, universe. I get you're supposed to be all knowing, but I think you've gotten it wrong this time," I say, tossing my phone aside in disgust after reading my horoscope.

There's only one person I've had a recent conflict with, and the stars have one thing very wrong. I'm not *itching* to do anything with him, least of all apologize.

I'll deal with that little bit of advice later. For now, I'm surprisingly eager to get back to yesterday's home project advice.

Refilling my coffee, I grab my tape measure and head out to the front patio to take a few extra measurements for the greenhouse. My conversation with the mysterious Archer last night aside, I have no intention of abandoning the greenhouse project for a rooftop fence.

The fact that yet another plant has been nibbled on, its flowers all but decimated, renews my commitment.

Lillian's yard—*my* yard for the next several months—is spacious by townhouse standards. There's both a paved patio and small grassy area. Even still, there's not exactly a ton of room to work with. Most of the space extends outward in a walkway leading toward the cute little gate marking the entrance to her property. And what little space is available off to the side she's set up as an outdoor dining area.

I've considered putting the patio furniture in storage, and since we're nearing the end of "dining alfresco" season, using that space for the greenhouse instead. But then I had another idea, one I like better . . .

A *vertical* greenhouse.

I read an article not long ago about the growing popularity of vertical *farming*, so I figure it can't be that hard to implement that same approach on a smaller scale.

Currently Lillian's plants are in a bunch of mismatched pots lined up against a wall of ivy on the right side of the property. I've never given much thought to what's on the other side of the ivy. But now I know what, and who, lives there. And even as I take all of my measurements to determine the optimal footprint for my vertical greenhouse, my gaze keeps cutting to that ivy wall.

Finally, curiosity gets the best of me and I let the tape measure release with a snap. I walk over to the ivy wall and gently wiggle a finger beneath the leaves, only to find it's not a wall at all. Instead of hitting a firm layer—brick, perhaps—my finger pokes through to the other side—

Someone flicks my finger, and not particularly gently.

"Ow!"

"Morning, Randy." Archer's voice sounds just as impassive in the morning as it does in the evening, as though he can *just* muster the bare amount of energy for a social interaction. "Sleep well?"

"Not particularly," I say to the wall of ivy. "My usually peaceful nighttime routine was knocked askew by a surly interloper."

"Hmm." He makes a bored humming noise. "I can relate. I have a noisy new neighbor."

"Noisy!" I exclaim. "I have never been accused of being noisy in my life!"

"You're yelling, Randy."

I narrow my eyes, inhaling for patience as my thumb flicks repeatedly at the metal tab at the end of the tape measure.

Unfortunately, Gemini Miranda has very clear marching orders for the day, and they do not involve strangling annoying artists with said tool.

. . . Take the first step by mending fences with someone you've had a recent conflict with . . . Their role in your life is not what it first seemed . . .

"Ugh. Fine," I mutter.

I head toward the front gate at the front of the yard. The wooden gate was probably once white, but most of the paint has chipped off, and the latch dangles uselessly, one strong breeze away from falling off completely.

Perhaps that should have been my home project; it's a good deal easier than my vertical greenhouse ambitions.

I walk the few feet to Archer's gate. In all the times I've visited Lillian over the years, I've never given much thought to the neighbors. I've gotten the sense she's on good terms with them, but she's never mentioned names. Certainly not *his* name.

His gate is in slightly better condition than Lillian's, but not much. I let myself in without invitation. His front yard is a mirror of Lillian's in terms of layout, though more bare bones—I doubt any red fairies live here. There are no friendly flowers or whimsical gnomes, just a few uninspired green plants, and . . .

Him.

I stop when I get my first non-blurry glimpse of Archer in the daylight, because he is *nothing* like he is supposed to look.

Something about his low, unhurried way of speaking made me think he'd be older, but he's only in his thirties. I can't tell exactly *where* in his thirties, though, probably because the bottom half of his face is covered in dark scruff that is more "couldn't be bothered to shave" than it is "look at my beard." His dark hair is wavy, a little too messy, maybe a little too long, curling down over his ears. It gives the same message as his facial hair:

Couldn't be bothered.

He's wearing faded jeans, a no-frills white tee, his feet bare. Add the chipped mug in his hand and the man should look slovenly—but somehow, on him, it translates to a very bedroomy vibe.

I suppose it could be . . . sexy. If you were into that sort of thing. Which I am not.

"Should I turn around?" he asks, idly lifting the mug to his mouth and taking a sip. His fingers are long and tan, making me wonder if his recent trip was to somewhere sunny.

"Turn around?" I repeat.

"You know. Give you a nice long look at the back side as well?"

I give an intentionally dismissive little sniff. "I suppose it's understandable you'd want to flatter yourself. If not you, then who?"

The corner of his mouth twitches slightly in a not-quite smile, and he takes another sip from his mug. His eyes are a dark blue, and completely unreadable as he gives me an un-subtle once-over.

I'm half braced for some sort of insult, given that I'm not yet showered. I'm wearing the same oversized sweater as last night, my hair's in a limp ponytail, and I've misplaced the *cute* glasses I wear each morning before putting in my contacts, so I'm wearing an old pair, which are a little too big for my face, and with an outdated prescription to boot.

Not so outdated, however, that I can't see he's not exactly dazzled by my appearance, and that my bedroomy vibe is not quite as alluring as his.

"You always spend your mornings like this?" I ask. "Lurking about, hoping a finger will poke through the ivy wall so you can startle your neighbor?"

"*I'm* not the one doing the poking," he says. "And yes, I do enjoy starting my mornings in the outdoors. Or, I did. Lillian's not nearly as loud as you."

I frown. "Again, I am not noisy or loud."

"You talk to yourself."

"I do not."

He sips his coffee and says nothing as he continues to study me.

Refocusing on my cause, I take a deep breath. "So. Archer. Apparently, we're meant to mend fences."

His eyebrows go up. "We're meant to? According to whom?"

Damn. I do appreciate a man who drops a grammatically appropriate *whom*.

"My horoscope," I say, lifting my chin and daring him to mock.

He accepts the dare because his eyes roll. "Oh no. You're one of those."

"One of *those*?" I ask, sounding awfully affronted for someone who just a few months ago might have thought the same thing, if not have been rude enough to say it aloud.

"Sorry," he says, sounding not regretful in the least. "By all means, mend fences. I'm happy to hear your apology."

"*My* apology? For what?!" I exclaim, forgetting all about my horoscope's gentle lecture.

"You tell me." Archer shrugs. "You're the one who thought there was a fence to mend. I didn't realize we had beef."

I wrinkle my nose. "Beef. Do people still say that?"

He sips his coffee again. "Do I look like I'm stressing over whether or not my vocabulary is current?"

"You look like someone who isn't stressing whether his haircut is current."

Archer cocks his head to the side, lifting a finger to his ear. "Did you hear that?"

"Hear what?"

"That was our fragile fence. Splintering further."

"Only because you keep hammering it with ill manners."

"Says the woman who charged over to my front yard at 7 a.m. uninvited."

He has a solid point there, but I will not be admitting it.

"Let's start over," I say, forcing a smile. "Let's pretend we're meeting now for the first time, and last night never happened."

I walk toward him, noting that for a man who seems not to care about his appearance, he certainly smells good. Clean, but a little enigmatic as well. The sort of scent you can't quite put your finger on.

I extend my right hand. "Hi. I'm Miranda."

"Don't you mean, Dr. Miranda Reed, PhD?"

I narrow my eyes and he rolls his again before shifting his mug to his left hand and extending his right. "You have a rather intense gaze, Randy. Are you always so serious?"

The handshake is meant to be perfunctory, more about the symbolism than contact itself, so I don't appreciate in the slightest the little of crackle of awareness when his much larger palm closes around mine.

Startled, I lift my gaze to his, and his blue eyes narrow ever so slightly. "What else did your horoscope have to say? You don't seem the type, by the way."

"What type?"

"The woo-woo type. Aren't doctors supposed to be logical? Not think the moon determines our mood, or whatever?"

I tug my hand away, which takes a second longer than it should, because his fingers take a bit too long to relinquish mine. Probably to annoy me.

"It's a new thing." I give my hand a little shake as I try to sort my thoughts, ignoring the way he notices and gives another of those half smirks at the gesture.

"What's new?"

"Reading my horoscope. *Following* my horoscope," I say, then order myself to stop talking before I tell this annoying stranger my entire story. Especially the recent, painful bits.

"Ah. Any chance you can leave me out of it?"

"Is this your vibe, or just your morning and late-night vibe?" I ask, waving my hand over him.

"What?"

"This indifferent 'life bores me' routine."

"Ah," he says again. "Just my sparkling personality, I'm afraid."

"How pleasant for everyone around you." I frown at him. "My horoscope says we're supposed to have a shared goal. Perhaps that goal should be avoiding each other."

"Love it. Stay off my roof, and we'll have a deal."

"*My* roof," I retort, crossing my arms. "I was wrong. You're apparently not the one my horoscope was talking about, because I'm not itching to make harmony at all."

"We could make something else," he says, dropping his voice and giving me a once-over that's a little more lingering than before.

"Gross," I mutter.

He grins, looking the least bored I've seen him so far.

"By the way, I'm starting a project over there." I point toward my yard. "And I don't know what the hell I'm doing, so if you hear anything that sounds like I've cut my arm off while trying to build a greenhouse, I'd appreciate it if you could overlook our differences and call 911."

I'm walking toward his front gate as I say this, but when he doesn't reply at all, not even sarcastically, I glance back. "What? No snarky comment?"

Archer tips back his mug, finishing his coffee, then gives me a resigned look. "My grandfather owned a landscaping business."

I blink. "Okay?"

He sighs. "His specialty? Building greenhouses. I used to

help him every summer. I also can't keep the damn rabbits away from my basil." He jerks a thumb over his shoulder toward some sad-looking plants.

"And?"

Archer makes a pained expression. "I think we've just found our 'shared goal.'"

VIRGO SEASON

*New Moon in Pisces today, dear Gemini. You'll find
yourself dabbling in a handful of firsts. Indulge in
experimental spontaneity as long as you don't use
these moments as a distraction from your most
essential purpose today: there's a conversation or
phone call you've been putting off. Today is the day.*

You're putting that in the wrong place," Archer says as I
start hammering a nail into a board.

I huff in frustration. "This is where you told me to!"

"No." He comes toward me, lifts my hand holding the nail,
and moves it the *tiniest* bit to the left. "*That's* where I told
you to."

I make a disgruntled sound and tug my hand away. He lets
his hand drop, but doesn't move, looking down at me. "You
don't like people telling you what to do."

"Does anyone?" I shoulder him aside, out of my personal
space.

Archer steps back but crosses his arms, tilting his head to

the side, which, over the past couple of days, I've noticed is his habit when he's assessing something. Or someone. Usually me.

I recognize it well. Growing up surrounded by scientists, I recognize someone intently studying a subject. I'd never thought about the fact that artists might intensely study something in the same way until now.

"You miss it?" he asks after a moment.

"What?" I give him a wary look out of the corner of my eye as I line up my hammer with the nail. We've been at this project for a couple of days now, and though I've gained quite a bit more confidence than when we started, hurling a hammer in the general vicinity of my fingers still makes me nervous.

"Teaching. Telling other people what to do."

I slowly lower my hammer and turn to face him, eyes narrowed. "How'd you know I was a teacher?"

"Google. And don't get prissy; I know you googled me, too."

I scoff. "How do you know that?"

He lifts an eyebrow.

"Okay. Fine. Not that it told me anything," I mutter. "You're as famous for being reclusive as you are for being an artist."

"Thank you."

"It wasn't a—" I huff. "Never mind."

I lift the hammer and nail again, but just as I'm about to swing the hammer, he moves toward me, moving my hand a bit to the left once again.

"Just mark it for me already," I say, exasperated.

He raises his hand to his head, pulls out a piece of charcoal that he seems to keep tucked behind his ear more often than not, and adds a tiny X to the right spot.

"I'm gonna get a beer. You want one?"

"Yes, because that goes so well with woodwork."

"So take a break. It's about to rain again."

I glance up, and sure enough, the skies are darkening. It's been a stormy past couple of days, mostly at night, which is why Archer and I haven't had a chance to resume our battle for the roof. The rain takes care of watering the Buzzes *and* prevents him from taking his easel out.

"You're right, but—hey!" I protest when I see he's heading into my front door instead of going back to his house. "If you want beer, you won't find it in there. Also, you're way too comfortable inviting yourself in!"

He's already gone, and I roll my eyes and follow him.

For the past couple of days, we've been building the greenhouse in my front patio area, and though Archer didn't seem to be overstating his expertise, I'd vastly overestimated my own. It pains me to admit it, but book smart most definitely doesn't translate to building stuff with my hands.

And to be fair . . .

I wouldn't say Archer has been *patient*, exactly, but he hasn't been as much of a jerk as he could have been.

Perhaps because he's taken our joint project as an invitation to make himself perfectly at home in my home, helping himself to fridge contents, the bathroom, and my TV when his alma mater's football game had been on.

"Hey. I mean it," I say, following him inside. "You're welcome to the wine, but I don't have any—"

I skid to a halt, finding him leaning against my kitchen counter sipping a beer. "Where'd that come from?"

He nods toward the fridge. "Brought them over this morning. Lillian gave me a key a couple years ago."

"I . . . what? Where was I?!"

He shrugs. "In the shower, I think."

I stare at him. "We are so not close enough for that kind of neighborly relationship."

Instead of replying he picks up a book off the counter: *The Complete Astrology Guide for Beginners.*

"But close enough that I'm ready to hear about this now," he says, giving the book a little waggle before tossing it back down. The book is massively thick, as are all my astrology books, and makes a distinct thump.

I wrinkle my nose in hesitation, and Archer reaches back, opening the fridge and pulling out another beer. He pops the cap and slides it across the corner to me.

I glance at it, then at the clock. I don't love beer. It's only 1 p.m., and yet . . .

I shrug and take a sip. An experimental first indeed, but not an unpleasant one.

"So?" Archer thumps the astrology book. "What's the story here? If I'm famous for being reclusive, *you're* famous for being smart. And logical. In fact, I even found a clip of you denouncing this stuff."

I take another sip of beer. "Your googling was *awfully* thorough."

He shrugs and looks away.

"Mine was as well," I say, leaning my elbows on the counter. "You may be a loner, but that's only fueled the curiosity. And the rumors."

He grunts and takes a sip of beer, not looking at me.

"For example," I say, beginning to count on my fingers. "I know that you got your start rather modestly in charcoal, but recently have exploded onto the scene with a Tokyo series done in acrylics. Much fanfare, blah-blah-blah. But before you did the art thing, you went to law school. That's an interesting bit.

Oh, but not as interesting as your high-profile engagement to Willow Dunn, which was called off *just* days before the wedding."

"For someone who's supposed to be smart, you're sure into celebrity gossip."

"Aha!" I point at him. "So you admit you're a celebrity."

"*Willow* was the celebrity," he says tersely. "I like to be left alone."

"Then why did you want to marry an actress? Not exactly low profile."

"I met her at fundraiser at the Getty when I was in LA. She was hot," he adds after a moment.

"You proposed because she's pretty? And why did you guys call it off?" I can't help from asking. "Nobody seems to know why."

"Not all details are meant for public consumption, Dr. Reed. You should know that better than anyone."

I narrow my eyes. "How do you figure?"

"Well. Someone's put together a pretty thorough Wikipedia page on you, but it doesn't say shit about . . ." He uses his thumb to gesture at the stack of astrology books on my counter.

"Yes, well," I murmur, running a finger along the spine of *Beyond the Zodiac*. "I'm not sure my reputation can take another hit."

"Another hit? What was the first?"

"Nova denied my tenure bid. Probably only a matter of time until that little tidbit makes it onto Wikipedia."

Archer looks skeptical. "Is that interesting enough for Wikipedia?"

A surprised laugh slips out. "Most people offer condolences about my career going down the drain."

He looks at me for a long minute, then glances again at the astrology stack. "So, what's your horoscope have to do with all this?"

"I'm on sabbatical for a year. Not my idea. My best friend suggested I do a sort of *Eat, Pray, Love* thing. Basically quit my life and do something a little crazy. That's a book about—"

"I'm familiar."

I blink. "Really? Well. I needed a . . . reset, I guess. A break. Change. Whatever."

His thumb scratches at the corner of the label on the beer bottle as he watches me, then he straightens and nods. "I get that."

"Really?"

"Well, not astrology, no. I think that's all . . . well, doesn't matter what I think. But you've gotta trust your instincts sometimes. Do things your own way."

Pleasantly surprised by his openness, I smile. "So does that mean you'll let me read your natal chart?"

"Absolutely not."

"Come on," I plead. "I want the practice. All I need is your birthday, time, and location."

"Oh, well. Let me just dash next door and dig up my birth certificate. Can I get you my ID while I'm at it? Passport? Social Security card?"

"I get it." I hold up my hand. "You don't want to be nice and neighborly."

"I'm helping the world's most uncoordinated woman build a greenhouse. My neighborly patience has its limits." He flips through another of my astrology books, the one on planetary transits.

I watch him for a moment. "Are you still hung up on Willow? Is that why talking about her makes you so grumpy?"

He doesn't even look up.

"Probably not," I muse. "I read on one of those websites that has more ads than content that you've been dating some . . . I forget. Publicist? Agent? Some Hollywood person."

"Your horoscope have anything about you driving me nuts today?" he asks. "Because it just might be on to something."

"No," I say, unoffended, because apparently I'm getting used to him. "But supposedly I'm going to use a moment of experimental spontaneity—a *first*, if you will—to try to put off a phone call I'm supposed to make."

His blue gaze flicks over to me. "Let me guess. You've managed to come up with a moment and a potential phone call that could fit the horoscope?"

"Yes. *This* is a first, actually," I say, lifting the beer bottle and pointing at it. "I don't make a habit of drinking on Wednesday afternoons, and definitely not beer."

"And the phone call?"

I take a sip of the beer, eyes lifting to the ceiling as I sip so I don't have to look at him.

He chuckles. "Ah. A dude."

I stay stubbornly silent, and he shakes his head. "Come on, Randy. You've already creeped on my love life. Make us even."

I bite my lip, realizing that maybe getting a male perspective wouldn't be the worst thing ever, even if it's from the worst *source* ever.

"I met a guy a couple weeks ago. Christian. He sort of saved my life."

"Oh, Jesus," Archer mutters in exasperation.

75

"No, seriously! He pulled me out of the street just as a car ran a red light and was about to hit me."

"That must have been a challenge for him. From atop his white horse in all that armor."

"Mock all you want, but there was a moment. A click. A mutual one," I say before he can dismiss this. "He gave me his card and said I should call him." I go to the drawer where I've stashed the card and pull it out so I can prove it.

"Well, that's more promising than expected. I thought you were just waiting for the wind to blow him back your way."

I glare at him.

Archer flicks a thumb over the corner of the card. "So why haven't you called him? Is it because talking *about* him has made your voice all fluttery and annoying? God only knows what happens when you talk *to* him."

"Thank you. This is all *very* encouraging."

"I'm not really known for my pat-on-the-ass pep talks."

"I'm shocked."

He picks up the card. Studies it. Then hands it back. "Just do it already."

"I can't . . . I can't just *do* it. These things take planning."

"Nope. They shouldn't."

"But—*hey!*"

Archer swipes my cell off the counter, holds it up to my face to unlock it, and dangles it out of my grasping reach as he dials the phone number on Christian's card.

He tucks it against my ear, and I have a split second to register that enticing, mysterious scent of his before the phone begins ringing.

"Damn it, Archer, I don't want—Christian!" I say a little

too loudly when he picks up on the second ring. "Hello. Hi. Hello. This is Dr. Miranda Reed?"

"*Smooth*," Archer mouths.

I give him a glare.

"Dr. Reed!" Christian says. "When you didn't call, I started worrying I came on too strong . . ."

"Not at all. I was just . . ."

Waiting for my horoscope to give me the go-ahead.

"I was just . . ." I flounder. "Thinking."

Archer shakes his head with a sigh, then grabbing his beer off the counter with one hand, he gives me a pat on the butt with the other.

"What was that?" I hiss, covering the phone with my hand.

"Pat-on-the-ass pep talk," he mutters. "Believe me, you need it."

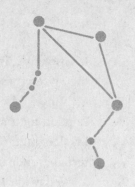

♎

LIBRA SEASON

The Sun is fully in Libra, and you'll be feeling that in a big way today, dear Gemini. Libra season is a great time to build relationships, and you'll begin one today with lasting impact.

Christian wants to see me.

Yay!

As a potential tutor for his daughter.

Yay?

When I'd told Daphne about the conversation, she'd sounded disappointed on my behalf. And she'd had a point. Would it have been a little more heart fluttery if he'd asked me to drinks? Or dinner? Or as long as we both shall live?

Kidding.

Mostly.

But the more I think about it, the more I like the way it's played out. I like that Christian seems to value my brain and field of study. Most guys' eyes glaze over the second I mention the big bang, and that had even included Daniel.

And the fact that he'd trust me to even meet his daughter?

It's romantic, in its own way. At least that's what I've been telling myself these past couple of weeks.

When I'd called him, Christian had been on his way to London for a weeklong business trip, and the week after that his daughter, Kylee, was traveling to Orlando to visit her maternal grandparents.

Today was the first available day for the three of us to meet, and I'm excited.

Okay, fine, I'm so nervous that I nearly threw up when I was brushing my teeth this morning.

Which is *ridiculous*.

I'm a thirty-one-year-old woman, I'm comfortable speaking in front of hundreds of people, I no longer bat an eye when I appear live on national television to talk about lunar eclipses.

But for some reason, a perfectly friendly businessman and his nine-year-old daughter are sending me into a tailspin.

It's just that . . . I have this eerie feeling that my horoscope was right about that meeting with Christian. That it was important. And this morning, the same day I'm meeting them, it just so happens I'm beginning a relationship with "lasting impact."

Even more eerie is that we were supposed to meet *yesterday*. Yesterday, when my horoscope had said nothing about an important meeting of any kind. I'd had to push the meeting to today after my dishwasher sprang an aggressive leak.

(Incidentally, yesterday's horoscope had mentioned a household emergency . . .)

Even if I wasn't committed to living my horoscope life as purely and fully as possible, the coincidence level of it all feels high.

To tame the butterflies, I've tried to shift my focus from Christian to Kylee, and the prospect of tutoring her.

Although academia was always my goal, I've never really considered teaching children. Or even high school students. It was always going to be *Dr.* Reed, always college students, always at a prestigious college . . .

Which I realize makes it sound like I was a precocious child likely to turn into an elitist, insufferable adult. I'm working on that last part.

But the point is that teaching *kids* has never been on my radar. And now that the seed's been planted, I can't stop thinking about it. The prospect of being able to shape a young mind, to foster her excitement about physics, promises a completely different sort of satisfaction than I'm used to.

A couple of minutes ahead of their scheduled arrival, I do a quick scan of the kitchen, making sure my astrology books are tucked well out of sight. As much as I'm trying to own the whole Horoscope Project thing, I just can't bring myself to introduce a child to the concept of being a Scorpio, or whatever she is, until she understands first and foremost that it's a constellation in the southern celestial hemisphere, nestled near the center of the Milky Way. I want her to understand what it *is* before she decides to take the leap of faith that it has any bearing on her life here.

Of course, I have to get hired first.

The doorbell rings just as I'm tucking the moon chart I've started keeping on the refrigerator into a drawer.

I open the door to father and daughter, and . . .

Holy butterflies.

He's better than I remembered. So much better. And the connection when his eyes meet mine feels even more charged.

A little unnerved by my own reaction, I force my attention to his daughter.

Kylee is cute in a wide-eyed, serious kind of way. She has long dark curly hair pulled into a drooping ponytail, huge blue eyes, and braces.

"Hi there! You must be Kylee," I say, deliberately focusing my attention on the girl to stop my gawking.

"Obviously. Did you think *he* was Kylee?" she asks with a tilt of her head, though there's a noticeable lack of snottiness, just a genuine curiosity over my stating of the obvious.

Her father lets out the tiniest of sighs. "Kylee."

She looks up. Blinks. "What?"

I smile to reassure them both that I take no offense and shift my gaze back to the handsome man in my doorway. "Come on in. Thanks so much for the last-minute reschedule."

Christian smiles again. "Not a problem. We're just excited that we could meet with *the* Dr. Reed."

I raise my eyebrows, and he smiles, meeting my eyes. "I did a bit of research."

"Ah yes. My infamous Wikipedia page," I say with a bit of a groan. I've never minded having such a public profile in the past, but now that I'm no longer in the public eye, it's strangely vulnerable to know that someone might learn more about me from the internet than from me.

Of course, since I'd done the same violating creep on Archer, I can't get too annoyed.

"So, since I'm on sabbatical right now, I'm thinking we skip that Dr. Reed thing and go with just Miranda?" I say, looking up at him.

And then I feel it. Something happens with my eyelashes.

Did they just . . . *flutter?*

Oh god. Am I flirting?

The ever-so-slight eye roll from Kylee tells me that a) yes, I am, b) I'm not doing it well, and c) it's not the first time a woman's turned all melty in front of her father.

"So, you're into physics, huh?" I ask, trying to pull myself together.

The way that her eyes light up at the subject warms my heart a little, reminding me of a long-ago Miranda who loved the subject for the sake of it, not as a career path.

"*Totally*," she says. "But my school's science program sucks.

"Stinks," she amends quickly after a look from Christian. "The only thing we learned are the planets of our solar system."

"As if that's the only one," I scoff.

"Right?!" Her voice is full of enthusiasm that tells me we're going to get along just fine. "My teacher didn't even know what I meant when I asked her about the spiral arms!"

Christian blinks once, and I smile at him. "Milky Way stuff."

"Ah. I love candy bars! I know, I know," he says, making a calm-down motion with his hands to a scandalized Kylee. "No more dad jokes."

"He tells them a lot," Kylee says.

I don't mind.

"So, anything in particular you're wanting to learn?" I ask her.

"Well." Kylee tightens her ponytail. "I looked up the curriculum for your The Universe course online. That sounds like an okay place to start."

"Honey, Dr.—Miranda teaches college students. I think—"

"No, no, Kylee's right again," I interrupt, smiling. "That's a great place to start."

Bright as Kylee seems, I'll likely need to adjust the actual textbooks to something more age appropriate, maybe simplify the subject matter a bit. But there's no reason I can't structure the lesson plan in the same way.

"So, how many days a week are you thinking?" I ask, directing the question to Christian, hoping that my eye contact is normal and not adoring.

"Five days," Kylee says quickly.

He gives her a telling look. "You have soccer Monday and Wednesday. Remember?"

The way her nose scrunches says she does remember but was hoping *he* forgot.

Christian's gaze returns to mine before he flicks his eyes upward for the briefest of seconds, all exasperated dad, but lovingly so.

"How are your Tuesdays and Thursdays?" he asks me.

"Wide open. The sabbatical thing, remember?"

"What's that?" Kylee asks.

It's what happens when your entire life falls apart around you.

"It's one of the perks of professor life," I pseudo-lie. "The idea is to take a break from the classroom and campus life to explore new ideas."

"What ideas are you exploring?"

"Um." I think of my ever-growing stack of astrology books tucked into a closet. "Star stuff?"

"She's dumbing it down for you, Dad," Kylee says, giving her father a comforting pat on the arm.

"I appreciate that," Christian says, and the way his eyes crinkle at the corners makes me melt a little. "Afternoons? Weekends? What's best?"

"I can work with either," I reply. "Whatever's good for your schedule. Or your ex-wife's, if she'll be the one dropping Kylee off."

I mentally cringe at the blatant curiosity in my voice.

"They never married. Mom and Dad hooked up in college. I was an accident," Kylee announces in a matter-of-fact way that makes it clear she has zero hang-ups about this.

Christian rolls his eyes good-naturedly. "Mornings are a little tricky for me, but I've got a pretty flexible schedule in the late afternoon."

"He's on the phone *a lot*," Kylee chimes in, doing an exaggerated impression of someone yapping on the phone.

"Thanks for that, Ky," he says, giving her a look.

"How's 4 p.m.?" I ask.

"Four is great," Kylee says, pouncing as though afraid the opportunity will disappear if she doesn't act fast. "Right? Dad?"

The way he looks at her makes me think he's wrapped around her finger, but happily so.

"Sure. I can drop her off at four. How long do these tutoring things last? An hour?"

"I have no idea, but I'd say let's make it two. If Kylee's down," I say.

Kylee nods eagerly, but before she can reply, there's a sharp knock at my front door. Before I can reply, it opens, and my obnoxious neighbor appears. "Hey, Randy, did you water the basil again? I already told you—"

Archer breaks off when he sees I'm not alone. "Oh. Hey."

"Hello," Kylee says with what I can only describe as a purr.

Oh, Kylee. You poor thing. If Archer's special brand of scruffy impatience is her type, she's got a rough road ahead.

I make introductions. "Archer, this is Christian and Kylee Hughes. Christian and Kylee, this is my neighbor, Archer. Who doesn't knock."

"I knocked," he says with a frown. "Did you not hear me knock?"

"Miranda's going to tutor me!" Kylee blurts out, her voice suddenly much too loud.

"Yeah? Hopefully not in botany. She sucks," Archer says, adding a wink for Kylee.

"Archer and I share a greenhouse," I explain to Christian.

I don't add that I'm sharing it *reluctantly*. But it was part of the deal we struck for him helping me build the thing. It's half his, although why he insisted on the provision, I don't know. He spends more time criticizing my care of the plants than anything else.

"Archer. I *love* that name," Kylee gushes as she stares with starry eyes at the brooding artist and royal pain in my side.

Poor thing's flirting skills are nearly as awkward as mine.

"It's his last name," I add, though I don't really know why. "First name is Simon."

I'd learned that from Wikipedia, too.

He catches my eye and glares.

Oh yeah, that's why I pointed it out. He *hates* the name Simon.

"An urban greenhouse. That's really cool," Christian chimes in. Then he sets his hand atop Kylee's head. "Come on, kid. Let's let Miranda get back to her day." He glances back at me. "If the rates we texted about are okay, and we haven't scared you off in person, how's next Tuesday work as a start date?"

"Perfect. And thanks so much for the opportunity," I say quickly, not quite ready to let this perfect specimen walk away before I've made an impression. "I mean, it'll be nice to stay sharp on the cosmos during the sabbatical."

Oh dear god.

Out of the corner of my eye, I see Archer's lips press together and roll inward, as though holding in a laugh.

I say goodbye to the Hugheses, managing not to say anything else to embarrass myself further.

Archer waits until I close the door and then leans a shoulder against it, smirking down at me. "So. That was . . . something."

I groan. "Was it that bad?"

"An improvement from the phone call. Barely. Just one little note—"

"What?"

His hand lifts to his face, fingers brushing the side of his mouth. "Right here. You've got some drool . . ."

I make a grumbling noise and turn to head back to the kitchen. "Since you're so good at seeing yourself in, I'm sure you'll have no problem seeing yourself out," I call over my shoulder.

"What about our basil?"

"It's fine. Go back to being a weird recluse in your weird studio!"

I actually don't know that his studio's weird, just that it's very off-limits, which he's told me about nine million times even though I haven't so much as set foot in his house, much less his precious studio.

Some of us have manners.

"I'm taking a day off. Not all of us gotta stay sharp on the cosmos," he calls after me.

I'm in the other room now, but I extend my hand and a middle finger in an unfamiliar, but very satisfying, gesture.

I hear him chuckle, and then the front door opens and closes once more.

I head straight for my laptop and begin researching books about astrology and relationships.

Suddenly I find I'm *very* interested to learn what the Horoscope Project will mean for my love life.

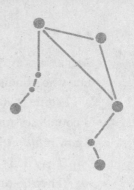

♎

LIBRA SEASON

Today will be one of relaxed contemplation. The Moon slips into Gemini tonight, prompting you to face emotions previously stifled. Don't fight the unexpected urge for openness, and don't try to go it alone. A listening ear will find you, perhaps from an unexpected source.

Already took care of them," Archer says, the scratch of his charcoal over his easel never pausing.

I glance over at his roof in surprise. "You watered the Buzzes?"

He shrugs. "Wasn't sure you'd be up here tonight."

"Really? Three-quarter moon in Gemini on a clear autumn night?" I glance up. "This is what I live for."

"Yeah, but it's also a Friday night, Randy. Typically, it's a popular one for going into the city, seeing friends. Hooking up."

"Hooking up?" I repeat in surprise. "Do you need me to give you a ride to the frat house?"

"You know what I mean. Dating. Sex."

He waggles his eyebrows at that last one, but I ignore him.

"Saw the kid yesterday bounding up to your front door,"

89

Archer says after a moment. "Seemed way too excited for someone who's doing after-hours science."

I smile. "She reminds me of me at that age. We've only had a couple sessions so far, but she's impatient that she doesn't know it *all* yet."

"They don't teach star stuff in school?"

"They do teach *star stuff*, but it's just the basics: the Earth revolves around the sun, the names of the planets, our solar system is one of billions, yada yada. They don't get to the *really* good stuff."

"You ever think of teaching kids? Like Kylee's age? Or was it always college students?"

I tilt my head, studying him. "You're awfully chatty tonight."

"Bored," he says, and though his tone matches his claim, I must be getting to know the man better than I realized, because I don't think it's the whole truth. I don't think Simon Archer is nearly as indifferent to the people around him as he pretends to be. I also get the sense that tonight he wants a distraction from his own thoughts.

"It was always college kids. I always imagined being a professor," I say, deciding to give him that distraction. "Though I'm surprised by how much I've enjoyed tutoring Kylee. It's refreshing to share knowledge with someone who's interested in the actual subject matter, rather than her GPA. All she cares about is how *cool* the sky is."

I tilt my head up and look at said coolness. "Which, in turn, helps remind *me*. When you're in a big lecture hall, sometimes you forget the wonder of how big the universe is, how tiny we are. And how the more you learn, the more you realize you don't know. The quest for understanding becomes like an addiction."

I let out a little laugh when I realize I'm borderline babbling. "You were right that first night. I *am* noisy."

"Huh. Guess I'm getting used to it," he says, a little distracted, since as usual, most of his attention's on his easel.

I sit up straight and put on my best authoritative professor expression. "I've decided it's past time I get to peek at your canvas."

"Is it, now?"

I nod. "It's not like I haven't seen your work. The stuff you sell."

That gets his attention. He looks over, less than pleased. "When?"

"Relax. I don't barge into your house the way you do mine. But there are a couple news articles about auctions of your pieces."

He continues to gaze at me but says nothing.

"You're quite good." I set the watering can on the table and pull out one of the iron chairs to take a seat. I've brought some of the furniture up from the garden, since while alfresco evenings in the yard have ended, I like the idea of rooftop evenings being a year-round experience.

"Flatter all you want," he grouses. "But you're not getting a look at this easel. I told you before," he says, flipping the piece of charcoal between his fingers. "What I do up here is just for me."

"Do you prefer it?" I ask. "The charcoal over the paint?"

He apparently decides my *noisiness* annoys him after all, because instead of responding, he drops the charcoal into the little chipped dish he keeps on the stool and heads across his roof to exit back into his townhome.

I blink. It's rude, even for him.

And I'm a little surprised at just how disappointed I feel to be alone on the roof. Not so long ago, I was irritated at having my solitude interrupted by Archer's return from his travels. But somewhere along the line I guess I've come to enjoy these strange, late-night sort-of conversations with one of the more confounding humans I've ever encountered.

I settle into my chair and try to channel Miranda from a couple of months ago, who relished in the peaceful silence. Before I can find her, Archer's rooftop door opens again, and he reappears.

I'm surprised when, instead of returning to his usual station behind his easel, he walks past it and steps over the small gap between our two rooftops with a long stride.

It's a first. The space between our rooftops is less than a foot, but it's been an important divide of sorts, and we've never bridged that gap up until now.

I'm trying to sort out how I feel about this when Archer unceremoniously sets a bottle and two small mason jars on the table. He pulls out the second chair beside mine and pours a splash from the bottle into each jar.

Lifting one of the jars, he raps it against the second, which he then pushes toward me. "Cheers, Randy."

I lift the jar and take a sniff, recoiling slightly.

"What is this?"

"Michter's."

I blink.

"Rye."

I blink again.

He shakes his head. "Whiskey."

"I don't drink whiskey."

"You do tonight," he says, settling back in the chair and taking a sip from his own glass.

I take the tiniest of sips, unsurprised to find that it burns a bit.

But I'm a *little* surprised to find that the second tiny sip is a bit better. And the third . . . almost pleasant.

"Pace yourself," he says without looking my way. He's slouched down in his chair a bit so he can tilt his head back. "These chairs suck."

"They do," I agree. "Especially for stargazing. Lillian said I'm welcome to replace anything, but I guess I haven't really gotten around to it."

He doesn't reply, of course, but the silence isn't unpleasant. Quite the opposite. I'm surprised when he's the one who breaks it.

"You miss teaching," Archer says, idly swaying the mason jar in his hand.

"Is there a question in there, or . . ."

Archer shrugs. "Don't need to ask. It's obvious from the way you were going on and on."

But when he glances over at me, his gaze doesn't match his exasperated tone. It's piercing, seeing just a bit too much. I look down quickly at my drink.

"I do miss it," I admit after a moment.

"But?"

I take a deep breath, startled to realize there *is* a *but*. "But I guess I thought I'd miss it *more*. Or rather . . . I thought I'd miss the rest of it more. People outside of academia don't realize that teaching is just a small part of what we do. There's all this other . . . crap. Everyone tries so hard to pretend that it's only about the science, when really at least half your energy goes into keeping tabs on what everyone else is doing, and making sure you position yourself in a certain light . . ."

"That why you do all the TV spots and interviews? It lets you teach and skips all the snobby professor stuff?"

"That's . . ." *Huh.* "Very astute. And yeah, I guess, but it was at my peril."

"How so?"

I lift a shoulder and sip the whiskey. "My attention from the 'nonsnobby' stuff is why I was denied tenure."

"Is it?"

I pivot to glare at him. "Yes. Why, you think there was another reason?"

"No." He holds my gaze. "I think *you* think there's another reason."

I suck in a little breath then, because until this moment, I hadn't realized that he's right. And that there's been a sneaky thought lurking ever since Dr. Kowalski broke the news to me back in April.

I exhale. "What if . . . what if they thought my heart wasn't in it?"

He continues to hold my gaze. "Was it?"

"Yes," I reply automatically. "I come from a long line of respected, tenured professors. This has always been what I wanted."

He pushes his tongue into the inside of his cheek before taking a sip of his drink. "So. What happens next? You do this horoscope thing for a year. Give yourself a break from campus life, from being a scientist, and then you just . . . go back? To a life you didn't really like?"

"I never said I didn't like it."

He lifts an eyebrow. *Didn't you?*

"Let's talk about something else." My voice is noticeably prim and testy.

"Sure. How about Dreamy McDaddy?"

"Pardon?"

"The kid's dad? The guy you can't put a straight sentence together around? He's your knight in shining armor, right?"

"Christian," I say, and it *does* come out a bit dreamy, like a tween girl with her first crush.

"Oh jeez," he mutters.

"Actually . . ." I frown. "I haven't really seen Christian. He hasn't gotten out of the car when he's dropped Kylee off."

"You're disappointed."

"And you're doing it again," I say, exasperated. "That annoying question-that's-not-a-question thing. Okay, no more talking about my career *or* my love life."

"What love life?" he asks, though there's no bite to it.

"Ouch," I say, though there's no pain behind it.

He smiles and slouches down a bit more in his chair so he can look upward. "Teach me something."

"Sorry?"

He extends his glass toward the sky. "About the sky."

"Um, that's a huge topic."

"Fine. Tell me how you feel about the moon."

"I don't feel anything about the moon," I say automatically.

He sighs. "Randy. Okay, then. Tell me something *empirical* about the moon."

"That's another huge topic."

He looks at me, exasperated. "Are you this difficult to converse with on dates?"

"This isn't a date."

"Definitely not."

"But yes," I admit. "I would theorize I am this difficult on dates."

"You'd *theorize*?"

"Well, it's not as though I've had many recent data points on that matter."

"Have you tried?" he asks.

"To what, gather data points?"

"*Date*, Randy," Archer replies with no small amount of exasperation. "You know. Put yourself out there?"

I sigh. "Let's just . . . go back to the moon."

He looks back toward the sky. "Fine by me."

I take another sip of the whiskey, realizing I'm rather enjoying the beverage. "You want me to talk about it as a lifelong astronomer or as a reluctantly budding astrologer?"

"Surprise me."

"Well. The astronomer in me would explain that the moon is in the final stage of its lunar cycle. It's 270 degrees away from the sun tonight. We see half of it during this phase, always the right side, which is the side facing the sun. Results in a neap tide."

"A what?"

I smile, a little surprised how nice it feels to dust off this knowledge and share it. I don't teach it in my classes. "It's when there is the least amount of difference between high tide and low tide."

Archer doesn't reply, but somehow I know that he's not only listening, but listening intently.

"Now, as far as what that supposedly means for us humans, per astrology?" I continue, more reluctantly now since this topic is uncharted water for me. "The third-quarter moon is purportedly a time when we're to . . . reflect. Or something like that."

"Let go," Archer says, cupping his glass in both hands.

"Let go?" I repeat.

He shifts in the uncomfortable chair. "Last quarter of the lunar cycle. It's about reflection, yes, but also release. Letting go of something that's no longer working, even if it's just a mindset."

I stare at him. "Why, Simon Archer. You have *layers*."

He glances over with a warning look, and I smile, but don't tease him further.

"You ever keep a journal, Randy?" he asks after a few minutes of silence.

"Not until recently," I say, surprised by the question. "I've been tracking all the horoscope stuff, though I try to be more academic about it than, you know . . . *dear diary*. Why?"

He jerks his chin in the direction of his easel on his roof. "These moonlight sketches. They're . . . you know."

"They're your journal," I say, understanding.

"I guess. Just with images instead of words."

"Explains why you won't let me see them," I muse, realization dawning. "I understand."

He makes a grunting noise that might be a thank-you.

"Do you prefer it?" I ask, shifting my weight to the side of my hip so I can study him. "The drawings up here, versus the painted pieces you sell?"

He sips his drink, seeming to let the whiskey roll over his tongue before he swallows. "Maybe. But nobody wants to buy charcoal drawings done in the moonlight."

"But the other painted stuff. That sells well?"

"Acrylics," he says. "I paint mainly with acrylics, and . . . yeah. I do okay."

"Your pieces are very beautiful," I say. "Even seeing them online rather than the real thing, they're quite . . . vivid."

He lifts a shoulder and I shift my weight again to look upward, since I sense Archer's nearing the end of his sharing, if I can even call it that. It still feels like progress, though to what, I have no idea.

After a while, I start to feel sleepy and contented, though the hard chair puts a serious damper on the latter, until finally I stand, ready to retire for the night.

"Thanks for this," I say, lifting my empty glass.

He nods.

I pick up the watering can and hold it to my chest. And then because the whiskey has loosened my mind and my tongue just a bit, I look down at Archer.

"My horoscope predicted this, you know."

"Rye whiskey in a mason jar?"

I laugh a little. "No. An unexpected connection. I must say, I didn't anticipate it would be with you."

The corner of his mouth moves. "Wishing it were with the kid's dad?"

"Maybe," I admit. "Though this wasn't half bad. Why, were you wishing I was . . . what's the publicist's name?"

"Agent. She's an agent."

"Aha! So there is someone."

He sighs. "There's a woman with whom I've had an understanding."

I stare at him. "Could you please be more vague?"

Unsurprisingly, he remains stubbornly silent.

"Okay, well." I give his shoulder a friendly pat as I pass. "I guess we'll count that as conversational progress."

"No," he says a little tersely, just as I'm about to open the door to go back inside.

"No, what?" I ask.

"No. I wasn't wishing you were her."

I smile as I head down the stairs. As far as Simon Archer goes, that was rather high praise.

♎

LIBRA SEASON

Mercury is in Libra today, and as it's your ruling planet, you'll feel the effect. Be prepared for a happy accident, a mistake that will initially feel uncomfortable, but is necessary for growth and moving forward. Resist the urge to take the easy way out, dear Gemini. A bit of risk and exploration will do you good.

Here we are," I say, carefully carrying two mugs back to my kitchen table, where my pupil awaits. "Two hot cocoas, extra marshmallows, and my special ingredient: just the tiniest sprinkle of cinnamon."

Kylee immediately fishes out a marshmallow, pops it into her mouth, and then extends a piece of paper my way as I take my usual chair across from hers. "What's this?"

"Let's see," I say, accepting the paper. I barely withhold the cringe when I see what she's been studying.

"That would be a natal chart." I try to say it matter-of-factly, and also a bit dismissively. As though it's not worth discussing. As though I'm not kicking myself for somehow leaving it out instead of putting it where it belongs: with the astrology stuff I hide for two hours every Tuesday and Thursday while Kylee's at my place.

"What's a natal chart?" she asks, not buying my dismissal. She snatches it back before I can discard it, peering at it in a way that makes my heart sink. Her expression is the same one I see when one of my students—well, former students—latches on to a particularly cool concept like quantum entanglement.

Only this isn't advanced science that Kylee's latched on to. It's an ancient belief that's been proven wrong by science time and again. My first instinct is to put on my firmest teacher voice, take the chart away, and refocus her attention.

But then a memory bubbles up of when I was about Kylee's age and at the science summer camp my parents had sent me to instead of Aunt Lillian's. During one of the stargazing sessions, I'd wished on a star, just as Lillian had taught me.

But I'd made the mistake of saying as much aloud.

A counselor had overheard and been swift to tell me that shooting stars were merely a small piece of rock or dust hitting Earth's atmosphere—and that, by the way, wishes weren't *real*.

The most acute emotion in that moment had been the embarrassment at being called out. With cheeks hot with humiliation, I distinctly remember resolving that from then on, I would make sure to learn the facts of something before speaking on it.

I haven't wished on a star, a penny in a well, or a birthday candle since.

And I wonder if that hadn't been the real wound caused then. Not the sting of embarrassment that faded in a day or two, but the loss of a sense of wonder, the squashing of the possibility of anything magic.

I find myself suddenly unwilling to play that role in Kylee's life.

My horoscope had promised a happy accident. This is it.

And I won't be taking the easy way out, brushing aside magic with cold facts. I close the book on the Coma Cluster lesson I had planned for the day and decide to lean in.

"So this is a natal chart," I say, scooting closer so we can both see the paper. "It's an astronomical map of the exact moment someone was born."

She squints. "Is this the moment *you* were born?"

"It is. I'm trying to learn how to read it."

"But there are no words."

"Exactly," I say. "But all these little symbols? They mean something."

"Like what?"

I smooth a hand over the paper. "Okay, so, you see this ring around the outside divided into twelve sections? Those are the constellations, or the zodiac signs. And all *these* little symbols," I continue, "these are the planets."

Kylee points at the symbol of the crescent moon. "But the moon's not a planet."

I smile. "Not as defined by the science community. The moon is not a planet by *astronomy's* definition. But in *astrology*, the sun and the moon are treated as planets. They're actually called luminaries."

"Astrology," Kylee says, testing the word. "That's what horoscopes are, right?"

"Well, actually, horoscopes are just a *part* of the study of astrology. For example," I say. "You know how when you talk to some people about *space*, and they can maybe name our solar system's planets, and they think that's all there is?"

She rolls her eyes dramatically. "*Oh* yeah."

"Well, that's probably how astrologists feel about horo-scopes. It's a tiny piece of a really big puzzle."

"Probably?" she asks, looking up at me with wide, curious eyes. "You don't know?"

"Well, I'm not an astrologist. I'm more . . . hmm. Do you know what it means to audit a class?"

She shakes her head.

"Well, on college campuses, you can sometimes sit in a class outside your field of study. You don't get a grade, but you also don't get any academic credit."

Her nose wrinkles as she blows on the hot chocolate steam. "So what's the point?"

"I used to kind of wonder that myself," I admit, poking at a marshmallow. "But that's sort of what I'm doing this year. Auditing astrology. Doing my best to understand it, even though it's not my typical field of study."

Kylee considers this, then nods before bending over my chart again. "What does it mean when each planet is in a dif-ferent zodiac slice of the pie?"

Her fingertip moves in a circle, touching each symbol in turn.

"Well, for example, here is the symbol of the sun, and the sun is in Virgo. That basically means that from the vantage point of someone here on Earth, the sun was crossing in front of Virgo at the time I was born."

"It's close to the line," she says, bending her head to peer closer.

"Yes, it's only one degree into Virgo. Just a *tiny* bit the other way, and my sun sign would be a Leo."

She lights up in recognition. "I know all about signs. I'm a Leo. August 3. That means I'm fiery."

I smile. "Quite probably. But all that means is on your chart the sun would be right about here." I point. "To really get the *full* picture, we'd need the rest of your chart. Especially your ascendant sign."

"What's that?"

"In astrology, it's the important one," I say, waggling my eyebrows comically.

She leans eagerly forward, far more excited about this than the science lesson we're supposed to be having. I know I should feel guilty, but it feels sort of nice to fuel this sort of creative thinking rather than squash it.

The facts will always be there. This kind of wondrous, open-minded thinking may not be.

"So what *is* my ascendant sign?" Kylee asks.

"I don't know. I'd need the year you were born, the city where you were born, and the time."

"Hmm." She bites her bottom lip and thinks. "I'd have to ask my parents about that."

"Well, I'd be happy to tackle that next time," I say, starting to put the chart away to shift gears back to what I'm actually getting paid to teach her.

Once again, she reaches out and grabs the chart, chewing her lip. "My mom's a Taurus, and my dad's a Sagittarius. That's why they never got married."

Oh dear.

I sip my hot chocolate, knowing I'm in potentially dangerous waters and need to proceed carefully. "Why do you think that?"

"I've seen the charts in my friend Emma's magazines," she informs me very matter-of-factly. "Taurus and Capricorn aren't compatible. But my stepdad is a Cancer, and that's why he makes her so happy."

When I don't immediately reply, she looks up at me. "Right?"

"Well." I take another sip of hot chocolate, trying to figure out how an astrologist would approach this conversation. "We can't forget that the natal chart is made up of a lot more components than just the sun. Which means we're made up of a lot more elements than just whatever personality traits are associated with our sun sign. So compatibility is dependent on a *lot* of different factors, even if just from an astrological perspective."

And the responsible adult in me can't keep from adding: "What's *really* important is that your stepdad and mom make each other happy. Regardless of what their charts might say."

"But charts *do* say something," she says, persistent. "About love compatibility, right?"

"Sure. There's a whole branch of study of astrology called synastry."

"Synastry." Kylee tries the word. "It can tell you if two people are meant to be together?"

"Um. In theory. You're awfully interested in this. You have someone special in mind?" I ask, wondering if this line of conversation all stems from a crush on her classmate.

Kylee nods very solemnly. "Yes. I want to find a girlfriend for my dad. His perfect match."

♎

LIBRA SEASON

The New Moon is in Scorpio, dear Gemini, making
this an ideal time to learn a new skill, perhaps
one you've been putting off out of fear of a new
direction. Proceed with caution, though; test your
new knowledge with low-risk endeavors to hone
your skills for when it really matters . . .

I'm sitting at the kitchen table poring over my astrology books when I hear my front door open. I don't even have to look up to know it's Archer, who's made a habit of stopping by whenever he feels like it. Which is often.

"Randy," he says by way of greeting as he goes to the fridge.

I tug the band out of my hair and rub at my scalp, which has been in a tight pony all day. "Did you do this with Lillian?" I ask.

"Do what?" He pulls a Tupperware with leftovers out of my fridge.

"Let yourself in. Pilfer her food?"

"Do I at least get points for not drinking directly out of the carton?" he asks, pouring juice into a glass he's grabbed from the cupboard.

"I can barely contain my applause. And you didn't answer the question."

He takes the lid off the container, sniffs, and then pops the leftover chicken Parm into the microwave. "I'm not great about remembering to grocery shop when I'm deep in the zone on a piece. But"—Archer drains the orange juice in three gulps before continuing—"since from what I can tell, your aunt subsisted on cigs, sherry, and smoked oysters, no. I did not pilfer her food."

"I asked her about you," I say, standing to get myself a wineglass from the cabinet.

He grabs the pinot grigio out of the fridge and wordlessly fills my glass, and I'm a little startled to realize how *natural* this routine feels. That it is a routine at all.

"Lillian declared you a 'charming mystery,'" I say, even though he doesn't ask. "I readily agreed with the mystery part."

"Hmm." He grabs a wineglass for himself, which is not part of the routine. Usually it's a beer, or rye whiskey, if we're up on the roof.

"She said that years ago, she met your fiancée a few times," I say casually, giving my wineglass a little twist, watching the liquid swirl.

Lillian also told me that she liked Archer's almost-wife quite a bit and was disappointed they hadn't worked out. What she *hadn't* known was why they hadn't worked.

And from the stubborn look on Archer's face right now, I don't think I'm going to find out, either.

He pulls the Tupperware out of the microwave. "You want?"

"No, thanks. Actually. Yeah," I say, realizing that dinner-time has come and gone, and I'm hungry. But he isn't distracting me from the fact that he's plating up *my* food. "Why not order takeout? Or delivery?" I ask as he divvies the leftovers onto two plates. "It's way better than what I can cook."

He shrugs. "I'm not picky about food when I'm working. It's just sustenance."

I lift my eyebrows. "And yet you grow fresh herbs. Thanks to my greenhouse."

"*Our* greenhouse." He hands me a plate.

"Fine, then why do *we* grow herbs if you don't care about food?"

He's quiet for a moment. "My mom's big into her vegetable garden. The herbs were always her pride and joy."

"You have a basil plant to feel close to your mom?" I pause. "I think that is just about the cutest thing I've ever heard."

He jabs his fork in my direction. "Tell anyone, and . . ." He draws the fork across his throat in a menacing way.

I mime locking my lips and tossing the key.

"What's all this?" Archer asks, this time using his fork to gesture to the books spread out in front of me. "Still on planetary transits?"

"Wow." I take a bite of chicken. "You managed to say that without even a trace of mocking."

He shrugs. "Other people are free to believe whatever fanciful crap they want. As long as it doesn't touch my life, I've got no problem with it."

Archer's attention is on his chicken, so I study him a moment over my wineglass. As blasé as his tone is, there's a sharpness there. A defensiveness that goes beyond just the usual derision.

"I think I finally got a grip on transits," I say, treading

lightly. "An astrological grip, I mean. As an astronomer, I've known about planetary transits forever."

"Am I going to regret asking what an astrological grip entails?" he asks warily, taking a sip of wine.

"You know, I know you don't care about this stuff. But you always ask. Why is that? Guilt? You feel you have to make polite conversation while eating all my food?"

He lifts a shoulder in a shrug. "Just seems like you process things by explaining them to people. It's like . . . your thing."

I stare at him a moment, a little unnerved by how spot-on that feels. "I'd never thought about it. But you're absolutely right."

"I know. So. Transits?"

"Right. At its most basic—the NASA definition—it just means that a planet passes between a star and its observer. So, if we see Mercury pass in front of the sun, that's a transit."

"And in your world?"

Years of conditioning nearly have me clarifying that NASA *is* my world, but the instinct isn't quite as sharp as it was even a few weeks ago.

"In astrology, it's still about the movement of planets, but there's meaning to the movement. Determined by the relationship of the current position of the planets and the location they were in at your birth." I pause. "You know. The natal chart. Which I need practice reading."

He gives me a knowing look. "Nope."

"Come on. All you need to do is give me your birth certificate. Or just give me the facts I need."

For a couple of weeks now I've been begging Archer to let me study his natal chart. I've done Daphne's, Lillian's, and my sister-in-law's. Emily is a sweetheart and had not only volunteered hers, but also promised not to tell the rest of my family.

But while the practice has been great, I want to read the chart of someone I haven't known for years. Someone about whom I don't have as many preconceived notions so I can do a clearer, more objective read.

Someone to practice on before I read the chart I really want to see:

Christian Hughes.

Ever since my conversation with Kylee yesterday, I haven't been able to get the concept of astrological compatibility out of my mind.

Archer drags his last bite of chicken through his sauce and pops it into his mouth. Then looks at my plate. "You going to eat that?"

"Yes."

He grunts and puts his plate in the dishwasher before going over to the table and picking up my latest read. "Synastry?"

"Relationship astrology," I explain. "It's essentially laying two people's natal charts atop each other to create a synastry chart, and seeing how those two individuals impact and fit together."

His jaw tenses and he tosses the book back down. "So, bullshit."

I'm about to take a bite but I freeze at the vehemence in his tone. "Raw nerve?"

"I just don't think two people's future together should be determined by anything other than their own free will. If two people like each other, if they make each other happy, that's enough. Or at least it should be."

"Okay. Now I really want to read your chart, because I

think you're a secret romantic. But also, stubborn. A Taurus, perhaps."

"Why don't you just keep your attention focused on Dreamy McDaddy?"

I wince. "*Please* stop calling him that. It's super creepy."

"What's his name again? Chris?"

"Christian."

"Are you and *Christian* a match?"

I decide I'm full and I slide my plate toward him after all. He picks up my fork and begins eating the rest of my dinner like it's the most natural thing in the world.

"I have no idea. I can't exactly ask him for his birthday, much less his birth time."

"Why not? You harass me for mine."

"You're different." I wave with my wine.

"How's that?"

"Well. You didn't save my life," I say sweetly, batting my eyelashes.

"Why don't you just ask the guy out already? He's clearly into your whole quirky vibe. He took an inordinately long time picking up Kylee the other day."

I narrow my eyes. "How do you know that?"

"Because while you and he were gabbing on your front porch, Kylee wandered over to my yard while I was getting the mail."

"Oh! I didn't realize."

Archer snorts. "Point proven."

I bite my thumbnail and study him for a long moment. "My horoscope says I'm supposed to pursue a low-risk endeavor today. To practice for a higher-risk one."

"Okay?"

I drop my hand. "I think reading your chart is my low-risk endeavor. Christian's is the high risk."

He groans.

"What if I promise to not mention a word about it to you? You said that other people's beliefs didn't bother you so long as it didn't impact your life."

Archer lets out a tired sigh. "I did say that. But the thing is, Randy, you read my chart, and even if you don't talk to me about it, you're still going to have thoughts. Those thoughts will annoy me."

"How can my *thoughts* annoy you?"

"Everything about you manages to," he grumbles, draining his wineglass.

He puts that into the dishwasher as well, then starts to move to the front door. I reach out and grab his wrist. "Archer. *Please?*"

Archer's blue eyes hold mine for a moment, then roll in a dramatic, impatient fashion.

Wordlessly he slips his wrist out of my grasp, but instead of ignoring my request, he grabs a pen and a notebook off the table. He scribbles something, then drops both pen and note-book in front of me.

I look down. In addition to the year of his birth, he's written April 10, 4:11 p.m., Denver.

"You know your exact birth time?" I say, surprised. He doesn't seem the type. "Off the top of your head?"

Archer shrugs. "One of my mom's favorite stories was how she wished she'd pushed just a little harder so that I'd have been born at four ten on four ten."

"Ah. Well, thank you. Seriously."

He shrugs and heads toward the door. "No big deal."

"Any chance I can get your mysterious lady friend's chart, too?" *Or your ex-fiancée's, while I'm at it . . .*

"Don't push it, Randy," he calls back.

I smile.

Later, watering can in hand and layered up against the cool autumn evening, I climb onto the roof, surprised but pleased to find Archer in his usual spot despite the cloudy weather and crescent moon.

"Okay, I know I said I wouldn't talk about it, but I lied," I say as I give the Buzzes their nightly watering. "Brace yourself for this, but I analyzed our synastry charts, and we are not a match made in heaven. Total disaster on nearly every aspect, in fact."

He makes a *hmm* noise that is either distraction or complete disinterest. Probably a bit of both.

I look over. "Is that devastation I hear in your voice?"

His teeth flash quickly in the darkness, a smile that I'm guessing was unintentional. "Just bummed I'll have to return the ring I've been carrying around in my pocket since the day we met."

I let out a dramatic sigh. "And I had to burn all the notebooks covered in *Dr. Miranda Reed Archer* doodles."

"Covered in hearts, I hope."

"Obviously." I smile.

I set the watering can down and pull off my top sweater, because apparently I've added one too many layers, and it's not winter yet. The thought makes me realize that in a month, maybe sooner, it might very well be too cold for these rooftop chats. I try not to think about that.

"In all honesty," I say, readjusting my glasses, which were knocked askew. "The reading of our charts was a point in favor of synastry."

"How's that?"

"Well, it's pretty obvious that we're not meant to be romantically entangled, and the stars confirm this. Point, astrology."

"How is that pretty obvious?" he asks, looking over and sounding genuinely curious.

"Well, for starters, you have a girlfriend. Sorry," I say quickly, because he gives me the same glare he always does whenever I slip and use that word. "You have a *person* you see when you're in the same city, which is not very often. Am I getting close?"

"You can stop fishing for details, Randy. It'll be a futile endeavor." He straightens and stretches, looking at his easel critically before turning to face me. He tucks the charcoal behind his ear. "So, you ready for the high-stakes move now?"

"Hmm?"

"You said my chart was low-risk practice for when it counts. You going to ask Christian for his info now?"

"Well, actually . . ." I look down at my feet, feeling strangely hesitant about next steps.

"I'll probably regret this, but . . . spit it out, Randy." He says this with more patience than usual, as though understanding my discomfort.

"Kylee just texted me a little bit ago. With her dad's birth information."

"You asked his *daughter*?" He sounds horrified.

"No! No," I clarify. "She's doing this all on her own. She wants to find her dad a girlfriend."

"Ah. She's playing matchmaker."

"Well, she didn't say she wanted *me* to be the girlfriend."

"How am I so much smarter than you about this?" he says, coming toward me, dipping his head slightly and rubbing his forehead. "Of course she wants you to be the girlfriend."

When he glances back up, I smile, because he has a little smudge of charcoal on his forehead.

"What's the problem here? Isn't everything marching along perfectly according to your plan? To your horoscope?"

"It's just . . ." I cross my arms, feeling vulnerable. "I feel like there could be something there. With Christian. But it's also important to me to see through this journey I've started. Trusting that the stars and the universe have a plan for me. Letting something besides my brain guide me."

"Are those two things incompatible?"

I swallow and meet his eyes. "They could be. Right now, it's an unknown. Schrödinger's cat. So, it's a paradox, where—"

"Yes, Randy. I know Schrödinger's cat. Until observed, a cat in a box can be both alive and dead."

"So until I read Christian's chart, he can be a match and not a match. But if I look, then I'll *know*."

Archer lets out a small sigh and steps up on the ledge of his roof toward mine, his toes just tipping over the side. I'm standing on the edge of mine as well, so we're face-to-face, his scent as unidentifiable and compelling as ever.

"Look," he says a bit reluctantly. "I'm the last person who should be giving romantic advice. I don't do the whole loyal, doting, one-partner thing."

"Not anymore, you mean. You were engaged."

"The fact that you're speaking in past tense pretty much says it all. But my point is, I don't think your hesitation about reading Christian's chart has anything to do with astrology."

"It has *everything* to do with astrology—"

"And I don't think you're afraid that he won't be a match," Archer says, speaking over my objection. "I think you're afraid that he *will* be. Because it means based on the rules you've set for yourself for this year, you'll have to put yourself out there. That's the part you're scared of."

I swallow loudly because his words feel uncomfortably . . . true.

"Well," I say after a long pause. "I guess there is some good news to all this."

"What's that?" he asks.

"It's just . . . No matter what his chart says, there's no way he and I can be more incompatible than you and me. That's something, right?"

I don't realize I've reached out to touch him until my thumb absently rubs the smudge on his forehead. Startled by the contact, even though I initiated it, my gaze drops from his forehead to his eyes, finding him watching me intently.

"Yes, Randy," he says a little gruffly as I let my hand drop. "That's definitely something."

An hour later, I look down at my and Christian's natal charts.

To say that the universe has given its blessing would be an understatement. If my various references on synastry are even close to accurate? He and I are almost a perfect match in nearly every way.

In fact, astrologically speaking, Christian Hughes is basically *made* for me. Among other things, his Jupiter is in Libra in the fifth house, which apparently rounds my love language. And he's a Sagittarius rising *and* sun, which is my seventh-house ruler.

I press my lips together, wondering why the giddy feeling I'm expecting feels a lot like apprehension.

Then I scowl. It's Archer's fault. Archer, who basically called me a chicken.

To prove him wrong, I pick up my phone.

And ask Christian Hughes on a date.

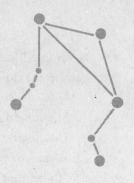

♎

LIBRA SEASON

Big change is on the horizon, and the anticipation of
it will have you feeling adrift in your own thoughts.
Your judgment and intuition are a bit hazy today,
dear Gemini. Trust a friend to get you through it.
They'll be able to see the situation with
a clarity you currently can't.

think I'm going to vomit," I say, setting a hand to my stomach. "Maybe I should cancel."

"You're not going to cancel," Daphne says firmly as she continues rifling through my closet. "And that barfy feeling is just butterflies. Before a first date, butterflies are a *good* thing, trust me."

Since I've been out of the dating game a good while longer than my best friend, I probably should trust her. But knowing butterflies are a good omen doesn't make them any more comfortable. For a fleeting second, I wish I could spend the night eating leftovers with Archer before bickering on the roof. No butterflies there, just comfy irritation.

Daphne looks over her shoulder. "This your entire wardrobe?

Never mind, stupid question." She blows out a breath and turns back to the closet. "Okay. Brown it is."

"I have colors other than brown!" I say.

She steps aside and gestures toward the closet. *Prove it.*

I stand and pull out one of my favorite plaid blazers. "See. This has red."

"Babe, that's like two percent red. The other ninety-eight is shades of . . . what would you call that?"

"Brown is a very flattering color on me," I insist.

She shakes her head in exasperation, but I'm quite confident that I am correct on this point. And I like what I'm wearing now. My dark brown turtleneck and khaki pants complement my medium-brown hair, dark brown eyes, and freckles in a pleasing, monochromic kind of way.

I'm apparently alone in thinking this, because while Daphne may seem the easygoing one, I recognize the stubborn set of that orange-red mouth as she continues to rifle through my limited clothing options.

Trust a friend . . . They'll be able to see the situation with a clarity you currently can't.

I go to the dresser and pull out a light blue cashmere sweater. "Better?"

"Perfect," Daphne declares, pulling a pair of navy slacks out of the closet and handing them over. "Now, let's talk shoes. No Birks."

"I wasn't going to wear *Birks*," I say, affronted. "I do own heels, you know."

"Yes, that you wear for public appearances and are very . . . professory."

She pulls out a shopping bag I'd barely registered until now. She reaches in and pulls out a shoe box, which I accept in surprise. "You bought me shoes? Exactly how bad is my wardrobe that you feel you have to supplement it?"

"They were on sale, they're in style, and they're *you*," she insists.

Skeptical, I pry the blue lid off the box, only to make a surprised approving noise.

"Right?" my best friend says, justifiably smug.

"These are . . . I love these," I say, immediately sliding on the loafers. I always love a good loafer, but these are cuter than my other ones. A rich mink brown with an almost velvety texture, and a thicker sole that makes them seem a little more stylish. I stand. "Ooh. I'm tall."

"They've got a little platform, so like a heel, but not," she says, giving a happy little clap. "Okay. Get dressed. Do your makeup—natural is *perfect*," she adds, catching my look. "Then meet me downstairs. We'll drink wine and talk about how Christian is going to fall madly in love with you."

Just like that, my queasiness increases tenfold.

A part of me truly is looking forward to the night ahead.

But the majority of what I feel is discomfort.

My last first date was ages ago, and it was with a visiting professor from MIT. We'd talked shop the whole time. Mentally, it had been downright titillating. But emotionally? Physically? The closest thing to chemistry that we'd shared was a mutual interest in spectroscopy. Somehow, I doubt Christian Hughes is going to have a vested interest in the study of the absorption and emission of light and radiation by matter.

I put on the outfit Daphne's picked and rummage around my limited jewelry collection until I find a pair of sparkly gold hoop earrings that I'd bought for a Nova University holiday party years ago and haven't worn since. I'm a bit more deliberate with my makeup, too. Black eyeliner instead of the usual brown, an extra coat of mascara. Even a bit of new coral lip gloss I bought on a whim a few days ago, per my horoscope's urging.

I take a step back and survey the result in the mirror.

"Not bad, Dr. Reed," I murmur to my reflection. I still look like myself, just not the boring, everyday version.

I reach up and tug the ever-present band out of my hair, releasing my usual low ponytail, and fluff my medium-length hair around my shoulders a bit. *Better.* I doubt Christian will faint at the sight of me, but it is nice to feel a bit *extra*.

I make my way downstairs, pausing when I hear the sound of a male voice. For a second, I think perhaps Christian's arrived early to pick me up, but as I get closer, I recognize the low voice as Archer's.

It's been stormy the past couple of nights, so I haven't seen him since our strange encounter on the roof when I'd rubbed a smudge off his face like . . .

Well, someone who's way closer to him than I actually am.

"Miranda Frances Reed," Daphne scolds the second I enter the kitchen. "How the *hell* have you not told me that you know Archer?"

I blink in surprise at the good-natured accusation. "You know each other?"

"Um, *I* know of *him*," Daphne says in a scandalized tone, handing me a glass of wine. "He's kinda sorta a big deal."

Oh. Right. The *art* world.

It genuinely hasn't occurred to me that Daphne might have known who Archer was, though I suppose I should have. Daph's a graphic designer by trade, but her obsession with art is practically a side hustle. She has annual passes to all the major Manhattan art museums, and even volunteers as a docent at MoMA on weekends.

I glance over at Archer, who's wearing a gray sweater, jeans, boots, and his usual sardonic expression. He takes a sip of his own glass of wine—Daphne must have poured him one, or maybe he just helped himself—with a raised brow.

"Why are you glaring at me? Did I commit some sort of greenhouse offense again?" I say.

"Nah. Hungry. But your fridge is practically empty."

"Because I knew I'd be going out tonight."

"Yes." He lifts an eyebrow. "I heard."

Our eyes meet and seem to hold for a second longer than comfortable, and I look quickly away. "There's eggs. Help yourself."

"I always do."

Daphne's head is ping-ponging between the two of us.

Archer gives me a not-terribly-flattering once-over. "You look different."

I roll my eyes. "Wonderful. *Different* is just what I was going for."

"You look fantastic," Daphne interjects. "So you two . . . you're . . . friends?"

"Neighbors," Archer and I reply at the same time.

"We have to share the roof space," I say, pointing upward. "And he helped me build my greenhouse, but only because the horoscope said I had to ask him."

Daphne's eyebrow lifts at Archer. "You said yes?"

He shrugs.

"Huh," Daphne says. "Okay, Archer, so as a huge fan, I have to ask: What are you working on now? Because that London series you did just . . ." She mimes a swoon. "If I'd had a few extra gazillion dollars to spend, that Bond Street piece would be on my wall right now." Daphne turns to me. "You've seen his work, right?"

"On a computer screen. Not in person. But I know that he paints . . . big . . . bright . . . paintings?"

And charcoal drawings at night. Just for him.

The art lover in Daphne appears horrified, and she looks quickly back to Archer. "Forgive her. She knows not what she says."

"Doesn't bother me," Archer says, refilling his now-empty wineglass and looking very much at home as he studies me. "So, you finally get the balls to ask out the guy?"

"I did."

Archer's eyes glint in amusement, though not in an unkind way. "Good for you, Randy."

"*Randy*," Daphne repeats. "Yikes."

"You'll get used to it. Miraculously, I have," I say, checking my watch. "I've got less than five minutes till Christian picks me up. Any and all advice is welcome."

"Be yourself," Daphne says automatically. "But except maybe, you know, ease him into the science talk." She makes a gentle wave motion with her hand. "Remember, some people think the big bang theory is just a TV show."

"Not anyone who's my potential soul mate," I say. "But point taken."

I look at Archer. "What about you? What do you have? Tips? Pointers? Advice?"

He lifts a shoulder. "Well, for starters, don't go throwing around the words *soul mate* on a first date."

"See, now I disagree," Daphne says, pointing her finger at Archer. "Didn't you hear about their charts?"

She makes a dramatic chef's kiss motion.

He rolls his eyes, but when he looks back at me, it's searching, though what he's looking for, I can't say.

The doorbell—which is extra loud, thanks to Lillian's failing hearing—interrupts her, and Daphne excitedly claps her hands. "Ooooh, he's here. Okay, I have to come meet him, because that's a best friend's prerogative. But *you*, stay," she says in firm command to an amused Archer. "No man wants to pick up a woman for a first date and discover a sexy, brooding artist making himself at home in her kitchen."

"Sexy and brooding?" I question, wrinkling my nose in confusion. "*Archer?*"

He gives me a cocky wink as Daphne pries the glass of wine from my hand and ushers me firmly toward the front door. "Trust me, darling," she whispers. "I'm right on that one. But let's just deal with one man at a time . . ."

125

♎

LIBRA SEASON

*Today you'll find your attention wandering in
unexpected directions. The curiosity is natural,
but be mindful of where your focus lands,
as it will guide your next actions.*

My date with Christian ended at a respectable time with a respectable peck on the cheek at the front door, but the emotional magnitude of yesterday apparently has taken its toll, because I sleep through my usual alarm and instead am awoken to my phone buzzing up a storm on my nightstand.

Sleepily, I grope for the device, unsurprised to see that the litany of text messages is from Daphne.

> Okay, don't even think about replying to this if you're not alone in bed. If he's there with you give him coffee, but not breakfast. Too much. If he's not there . . .

> How was it? I want details down to the food orders, and any accidentally-on-purpose physical contact.

> Also, he is cuuuuuuuute. Really cute. Like, Ryan Gosling cute.

Also, still a LITTLE mad you didn't tell me you knew THE Archer. And that he was hot. And also, what is going on with you two?

I groan, tossing the phone aside, and fold my arms over my face.

Way too many questions before coffee.

For a moment I let myself lie here, listening to the birds outside my window as I let my mind wander to last night's dinner date and . . .

I realize I'm smiling.

The butterflies that had been a permanent fixture in my stomach all day yesterday had vanished about the time he'd opened the passenger-side door for me. Though I'd been careful to steer clear of both science and astrology talk, there hadn't been even a whisper of awkward silence, just a pleasant flow of easy topics right up until he'd walked me up my front steps.

As for the kiss on the cheek?

A little unclear as to how I feel about that. Disappointed? Relieved?

Still, I'm pretty sure it had been more of a respectful *move slow* gesture than it had been about dismissal, because a second date is already on the books.

My phone buzzes again. A little more awake now, I pick it up. Another Daphne text.

He's more charming than I'd expect, given the circumstances.

I reply to that one.

I TOLD you he was charming.

Daphne: You did not. You didn't even tell me you knew him!

It takes me a moment to realize we aren't talking about Christian.

Me: Wait. Archer? Charming is not the word I'd use.

Daphne: I just expected him to be . . . awkward and weird.

Me: Don't worry, he has a slew of other negative qualities.
Curt.

Annoying.

Aggravating.

And okay, fine, also sometimes kind of funny. And kind.

But mostly annoying.

Daphne: Did I tell you one of the MoMA volunteers I work with is close with his ex? That actress Willow. She called it off just weeks before the wedding.

I sit up, a little more intrigued than I want to be. I read that. Lots of speculation about cheating or incompatible schedules, but neither of them has said a word about it.

Daphne: Look at you keeping up on your celeb gossip! And not even A-list!

Me: Can I tell Archer you said he isn't A-list? Actually, never mind, he'll for sure take that as a compliment.

Daphne: Maybe that's why they called things off? He didn't like the public lifestyle?

Me: Your MoMA friend doesn't know?

Daphne: GASP. Dr. Miranda Reed. Are you . . . fishing for deets on your neighbor?

Me: No! Merely curious about what makes him so grumpy. So back to Christian . . .

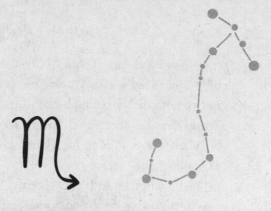

SCORPIO SEASON

With the Moon in Cancer, don't be surprised to find yourself in a domestic kind of mood today, dear Gemini. You may even discover previously untapped maternal or paternal urges. Explore them, but use caution: the Sun in Neptune opposition may make it difficult to discern fact from fiction.

That was *super* good, Dr. Reed. Thank you," Kylee says, pushing her plate away with a contented sigh.

The fact that her plate is scraped clean slightly soothes the memory of earlier this afternoon, when several near disasters in the kitchen had me worrying if I was destined for a lifetime of cooking for one.

Or two, if you count Archer's continued dedication to clearing out my leftovers.

"It *was* super good," Christian says, smiling at me across the table. Like Kylee, his plate is clean, though unlike Kylee, he's managed to keep the majority of the penne alla vodka sauce off his shirt.

"I'm glad you liked it. I admit, I had a bit of a last-minute scramble with the meal plan," I say, finally relaxing enough to enjoy a bit of my wine. "My original plan was a roast chicken, mashed potatoes, that whole deal. But then I remembered that Thanksgiving is next week. The meals seemed a bit similar."

"What are you doing for Thanksgiving, Dr. Reed?" Kylee asks politely.

"Just a quiet day at home," I reply. "My parents are headed to Arizona to visit my grandmother, one brother decided to go to London, and the other is with his wife's family."

"That's sad. All alone."

"Kylee!" Christian chides.

"Oh, believe me, I'm good with it," I say, smiling. "I like my own company, and I'll get to see everyone at Christmas. Plus, traveling is such a pain next weekend. You two are braver than me."

"When you meet my mother you'll understand that you have it backward," Christian says with a smile. "Saying no to her summons would have been the braver option."

When you meet my mother. Not *if*.

Isn't that . . . fast?

Though this—tonight's dinner—had felt fast, too. Christian and I have been dating, casually, for all of a month, and here I am cooking for him.

And his daughter.

Still, this one had been easier to get on board with, because it had been Kylee's idea, and even though it had been a pretty blatant attempt at maneuvering her father and me closer together, I hadn't had the heart to say no.

And tonight has been fun. It has.

But meeting Christian's parents?

That's next level. I haven't even slept with the guy yet. It's been hard to explain, but as much as I like him, I just haven't felt ready. Perhaps it's *because* I like him? Because our charts indicate Christian and I are perfectly compatible, and thus everything seems to *matter* just a little bit more . . .

Kylee looks pointedly back and forth between her father and me and apparently decides she's bored with us. "May I be excused to go stargaze?"

"Stargaze?" Christian repeats, startled.

"Dr. Reed does it from her roof. Right?"

I nod, but Christian is unconvinced. "I don't know how I feel about you up on the roof, Ky."

"*Please?* I'll be *really* careful."

"It's a clear night, which means my neighbor will be up there. He can keep an eye on her." I say it a little hesitantly, because it feels way too soon to be weighing in in any way on parental decisions. But I've also gotten to know Kylee quite well during our tutoring sessions and know she's neither clumsy nor reckless.

Christian blinks. "Your neighbor stargazes on the roof, too?"

"Eh, not really. He mostly draws." I wave a hand. "It's a whole thing."

"Huh. Alright, let me go see what we're dealing with, and then I'll decide," Christian says, pushing back his chair. He looks at me. "If that's okay?"

"Sure, of course. I'll start cleaning up." I start to gather the dishes.

He points at me. "Don't you dare. You cooked; I'll clean."

"Do you have a telescope, Dr. Reed?" Kylee asks excitedly as she pulls on her coat and zips it.

"Unfortunately, I do not," I say with a bit of regret. "I had a beautiful one, but when I moved to Manhattan for school at NYU, there was just too much light pollution. Not to mention a lack of outdoor space. I donated my telescope to a science camp so someone could make better use of it. You can still see a few stars, though," I continue. "The light from the city prevents any *proper* stargazing, but I'm excited to hear what you can identify just by using the naked eye."

"Okay!" Kylee says, already bounding toward the stairs.

"Be right back," Christian calls over his shoulder. "Remember. I clean."

"Absolutely," I agree. But the second I hear their voices heading up the stairs to the roof, I stand and stack the plates. I need something to do with my hands to keep my brain from going into overdrive, analyzing every moment of the evening so far.

I'm pretty sure it went well, but I'm out of my depth here with this homemaking thing, no matter what my horoscope says about my "domestic mood."

As far as the untapped maternal urge, I can't deny that I've felt an unfamiliar longing in that direction as well. The more time I spend with Kylee, the more I realize I enjoy children. Enjoy her.

And her dad, too. Christian is . . .

Every bit the Prince Charming he'd seemed that first day on the sidewalk.

He's polite. Charming. An effortless conversationalist. There's an *easiness* with him that is exceedingly pleasant. He even seems to be a wonderful father; Kylee clearly adores him.

But there is maybe just the tiniest part of me that can't stop wondering:

Am I following my heart?

Or my horoscope?

Which is aggravating as hell, because the entire reason I even started the Horoscope Project was to access that other, untapped, or perhaps long-buried part of myself. But lately, Aunt Lillian's parting warning before she'd gone to Florida is rattling in my head:

"Don't trade one set of rules for another."

The fact that Christian is a father only adds to the complexity. Kylee's been quite clear from the beginning that she wants to find her dad a girlfriend, and while of course nothing's been said explicitly this early in the relationship, Christian isn't the kind of guy who would engage in a fling, especially not with his daughter's tutor . . .

I turn away from the sink to grab more dishes and jump when I see Christian in the doorway.

"Lurk much?" I say, shaking out my damp hands and wiping them on a towel.

"You mutter unintelligibly to yourself when you're thinking," he says, moving closer to me with a smile. "Did you know?"

"It's been mentioned," I say, smiling back as he wraps his arms around my waist. I loop mine around his neck, the gesture still not quite natural for someone unaccustomed to physical affection, but he doesn't seem to notice or mind.

"Is it weird if I say I'm going to miss you while I'm at my parents' for Thanksgiving?" he murmurs, brushing a soft kiss over my mouth.

"If it is, I like weird," I reply.

"Hmm." He kisses me again. "I scared you when I mentioned meeting my mother, didn't I?"

"Not at all," I lie, and he seems to believe me, because he pulls me closer.

"Good. Because I can picture you all too easily coming with me and Kylee to Oregon for Thanksgiving to meet my parents."

"Oh. Wow."

I stiffen, and he laughs. "Don't worry, I don't mean this year. I know we're too soon for the meet-the-family thing. I just . . . I don't know, I saw you here, and realized I was bummed about the fact that I wouldn't get to see you this weekend."

"I'm disappointed, too," I say, forcing myself to relax.

"Alright," he says, with one last kiss before stepping back. "So, here's what we're going to do." He pulls me toward the table. "You're going to sit and drink this delicious wine that I brought. I'm going to clean up. And you can reassure me that the moody guy on the roof doesn't have a crush on you."

I let out a genuinely started laugh. "Archer? Goodness. No. I'm not sure Archer even likes me. Or anyone," I add after a moment.

"Do you like him?" Christian asks, giving me a faux-menacing look over his shoulder as he carries the serving dish to the sink.

"Depends on the day." I smile. "But no, not like that. Besides, he's got a girlfriend. Thing."

"A girlfriend *thing*. Color me intrigued."

I shrug. "I'm not really clear on the details. I think it's some modern, nonexclusive situation? From the bare-bones details he doles out, she's a high-profile agent who's in Los Angeles most of the time, but when she's here . . ."

He wiggles his eyebrows suggestively.

"Yes," I confirm. "I believe that's how it works."

Mostly I try not to think about it.

"Well, whatever works for him," Christian says amiably. "Just as long as he doesn't have eyes for *my* girlfriend."

I'm still wiping some grated Parmesan off the table, but at that I pause. "Your girlfriend. Me?"

Christian laughs. "I was aiming for subtlety, but perhaps I was *too* subtle if you have to ask who I meant."

"Sorry," I say. "Like I said, I'm—"

"New at this, I know." He wipes his hands on his pants and closes the distance between us, pulling me to my feet once more. "I'd love to be the one to help you be a little *less* new at relationships. If you're interested."

I think it over, then give a slow nod. "I'm interested."

"Good," he says in a satisfied voice, pulling me in for a kiss. And even as I try to lose myself in the pleasant sensation, I can't help thinking about that Sun/Neptune opposition today.

The one that's making it difficult for me to discern fact from fiction.

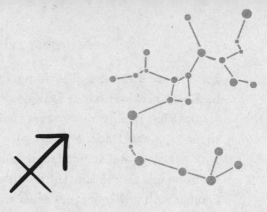

SAGITTARIUS SEASON

The threat of change seems to be knocking on every door today, darling Gemini. You'll feel as though you're looking at everything with fresh eyes, from old routines to relationships that are perhaps not quite what you've always believed. Try to embrace the discomfort: it's attempting to tell you something.

I've never been a big Thanksgiving person. I'm not *anti*, or anything; the holiday's always just felt like too much.

Too much pressure. Too much family drama. Too much food.

Growing up, we'd always spent it somewhere else. Grandparents', aunts and uncles' (and not the cool aunts and uncles like Lillian, but the uptight ones who wouldn't let you have pumpkin pie until you'd eaten the Brussels sprouts).

When the extended family had eventually scattered in my teens, my not-terribly-kitchen-inclined parents had taken to ordering a premade meal from the local grocery store. It must have been more for us kids' sake than their own, because there hadn't been even a whisper of a guilt trip when I'd stopped going home every year. Providing, of course, that I made it back for Christmas, which I always do.

But that means, more years than not, Thanksgiving is spent . . . alone. Daphne always goes to Michigan to spend it with her mom and stepdad, and Lillian has a long-standing tradition of a Caribbean cruise with her friends. I'm not close enough with any colleagues other than Elijah, and even his and my friendship isn't remotely at the level of warranting a holiday invitation.

In years past, I've spent the long, luxurious weekend all to myself to . . . work.

And I don't say that in a please-pity-me way. I've always loved it. I catch up on academic journals; I lesson-plan. I assess career goals. I grade papers, tweak exams. All while eating too much pie, because while I may not participate in most of the usual holiday traditions, I can certainly get behind the magic that is pecan pie. Until now, I have never been able to imagine a better way to enjoy a few days off.

But here's the thing about making work your whole life:

When your work disappears?

You realize just how empty your life really is.

And how alone you really are.

Halfheartedly I sit at the kitchen table and open *Predictive Astrology.* I've felt pleased with myself these past couple of weeks for having graduated beyond the beginner astrology books, perhaps even surpassing Daphne's knowledge of the field, at least in terms of facts.

But tonight, I can't get into it. Any of it.

For the first time since I can remember, I don't want to read. I don't want to learn.

I don't want to be alone.

And strangely, the absence I'm most aware of is . . . Archer. I haven't really registered just how often he's around until he's not.

I hadn't even realized he was planning to go out of town until I got a text message yesterday reminding me not to over-water his precious basil while he's gone.

I do that now, pleased to see that the plant is thriving, as are the rosemary, thyme, and sage. I pluck a sage leaf now and lift it to my nose, the scent reminiscent of the Thanksgiving food I won't be enjoying. Cooking for one had just felt sad, but all of the premade meals at the store yesterday had served a minimum of four.

Instead, I'd settled for picking up a pecan pie, which has always been a favorite.

In fact, maybe I'll just make that my dinner. At least it'll be Thanksgiving dinner adjacent.

I give the sage one last wistful sniff and go back inside. I've missed a FaceTime call from Christian.

I mean to call him back, and then . . . don't.

I'm debating whether red or white wine is the least-gross pairing for pecan pie when Lillian's too-loud doorbell has me nearly jumping out of my skin.

I check the peephole, and then open the door in surprise. "*Archer?*"

"Since when have you started locking your front door?" he demands, as though I've committed some crazy offense.

"Um, since a strange man started letting himself into my house?" I say as he nudges me out of his way and steps inside. "And I really only left it unlocked during the summer because it was easier to come in and out as we were working on the greenhouse."

He grunts in minimal acknowledgment.

"Happy Thanksgiving, by the way." I nod at the shopping bag on his arm. "What's that? You finally come to replace some of the food you've been stealing?"

He reaches out toward Lillian's octopus-shaped coat rack and pulls off my navy puffer coat, shoving it at me before heading toward the back of the house.

"Bring a hat with you," he calls back. "But not that ugly one with the stupid flaps."

"Those stupid flaps keep my ears warm," I mumble, grabbing the ugly hat in question, as well as a pair of mittens, since we're obviously going up to the roof like a couple of lunatics in the middle of a major cold snap.

I hear the door to the roof open and close, and then open again. "Two wineglasses, Randy. The nonfussy ones with no stems. Oh, and that pie."

I make a mocking salute even though he can't see me and, grabbing the glasses and pie, hurry up the steps before he can bark any more orders.

Archer is already seated at the little outdoor table, though in a rare show of politeness he pushes out my chair with a booted foot.

"Kylee told me that she and your guy were headed out of town for the holiday," he says, pulling a hat of his own out of his winter coat and putting it on. It's blue, and it makes his eyes look bluer.

"When did you speak with Kylee?"

"The other night. On the roof. She talks a lot."

"Oh, that's right. I see she's graduated from 'the kid'?"

Archer shrugs. "She informed me that addressing her as 'kid' was *supercilious*. I had to look it up."

"She's right. It's a little condescending."

He rolls his eyes and changes the subject. "Be useful. Unpack that."

I do as he says, pulling out two sandwiches. The logo sticker holding the parchment closed is from the fancy sandwich shop up the street.

"Lona's was open today?" I ask, surprised.

"She opens for exactly two hours every Thanksgiving night. Best damn turkey sandwich you've ever had," he says, standing and taking a long stride onto his roof. He comes back with an enormous basket.

"What is—oh!" I say, pleased when he pulls out a warm, thick blanket and hands it to me.

"Don't get too excited yet. We're sharing that," he says before pulling out a bottle of red wine. "Sharing this, too. And your pie."

I set out the sandwiches and some bottled sparkling waters from the bag, while he takes a foldable corkscrew out of the back pocket of his jeans and wrestles out the wine bottle's stubborn cork.

"I thought you were traveling," I say, nodding in thanks when he hands me a glass of wine.

"I was. But there's a blizzard warning in Denver. My flight was rescheduled three different times, then canceled altogether."

"That sucks. Your parents live there, right?" I say, remembering from reading his natal chart that he was born there.

He nods. "I'm hoping I can fly out tomorrow or Saturday. The leftovers are the best part of Thanksgiving anyway."

Archer sits down again, then I let out a little yelp as he grabs the seat of my chair and hauls me closer. Unceremoniously, he readjusts the blanket so both our laps are covered, then clinks his glass to mine. "Cheers. Happy Thanksgiving, Randy."

We both take a sip, then Archer gives me a thoughtful look. "Where are Kylee and Christian again? Washington?"

"Oregon. Christian's parents and sister live there. He's from there."

Archer unwraps his sandwich and takes a large bite. "So you guys, like, a thing, or what?"

"Hmm?" I say, distracted as I watch him wipe a bit of what looks like cranberry sauce from the side of his mouth with his thumb.

"You and Christian. Must be getting serious if you're cooking for the guy."

I nearly point out that I also cook for Archer when he shows up unannounced and hungry, though that's really just a grilled cheese or whatever I'm already planning to have myself.

"We're increasingly involved," I say, beginning to unwrap my own sandwich.

He snorts. "You sure know how to romanticize things, Randy."

"You're one to talk. You won't even talk about your girl-friend."

"Because I don't have one."

I roll my eyes. "Fine. What *do* you call the woman you've been seeing?"

There's a long pause. "The woman the gossip sites were talking about is Alyssa."

"Why do you never talk about her?" I ask.

He says nothing.

"Okay, so you don't cook for each other," I prod. "What *do* you do?"

He gives me a look.

"I mean, for *food*," I say a bit primly.

He flashes a quick grin, enjoying my discomfort. "So. Christian. You like him."

"Yes. I do," I confirm as I inspect the sandwich. "What's on this?"

He lifts a shoulder. "Roasted turkey breast. Cranberry sauce. Brie. Magic."

I smile.

"So?" Archer says as I take a bite.

I look over, surprised to see that he's watching me. "So what?"

"Can I come to the wedding?"

I choke a little on the sandwich and have to wash it down with wine. "Why so nosy about Christian?"

"Just being polite, Randy."

"Actually, being nosy is the opposite of polite."

He shrugs.

For a while we sit in silence, enjoying our sandwiches—which, to his point, does taste a bit like magic. The turkey is moist and flavorful, and the tartness of the cranberries keeps the Brie from becoming too rich and overwhelming. The bread is freshly baked, and heavenly.

"What made you do this?" I finally ask.

I hand him the last quarter of my sandwich that I'm too full to finish, and he accepts it without hesitation. "Do what?"

"This . . . picnic," I say, gesturing at the spread.

Archers swallows a bite of sandwich, takes a sip of wine. "I was alone. Figured you were, too. Not the way one should spend a holiday if they don't have to."

"That's surprisingly . . . thoughtful."

"Just had my software updated," he says, tapping his temple, then balls up the sandwich wrapper with a large fist and drops it into the empty bag.

"You know, you're not what I expected a professional artist to be like," I tell him.

"Oh god. Buy the girl a sandwich, and she wants to get deep." He glances over. "What'd you expect? That we all cut off our own ears, Van Gogh style?"

"No. I just mean that I've always thought there was a stark divide between art and science. Subjective versus objective. Emotions and intuition versus data and facts."

"I don't know that you're wrong on that," he says after a moment.

"And *yet*." I wave my finger at him. "You're the only artist I know and you're also very computational in the way you interact with people. Or at least with me."

Archer reaches for his wineglass and leans back in his chair, legs extended so his boots pop out from beneath the blanket. He sets the wine on his flat stomach as he seems to consider what I've said.

"I have them," he says slowly after a long moment.

"Have what?"

He sips his wine. "Emotions."

My head snaps up, and even though we're sharing a blanket, I'm still a little surprised to find him so close somehow, especially since the sun's just set. It's not as dark as it typically is when we're up here.

"I didn't mean that you don't have emotions," I say softly.

"I'm just saying that one can have emotions without spewing them all over the place," he grumbles. "You know that better than anyone."

I tilt my head to the side. "What's your moon sign again?"

"You tell me. You're the astrologist. Why? What does it matter?"

"Your moon sign determines your emotional makeup."

"Huh."

"I remember your sun sign," I say, snapping my fingers. "You're an Aries."

"Fascinating."

"Don't you want to know what that means?"

"I do not."

"But—"

"Randy." Lazily, he rolls his head in my direction, and since I'm still facing him, it brings our faces close together, though somehow it doesn't feel as awkward as it should. "What do you say you take a break from the Horoscope Project tonight? Just for tonight, be Miranda. Not an astrologist, not an astronomer. Just a woman who believes she makes her own destiny. Who doesn't believe the stars determine our personality or love match."

For a moment I only look at him, then I hear myself whisper, "Okay."

I feel a little shaken, though I don't fully know why. His blue eyes drop to my mouth for the briefest of moments before he looks away.

I, too, look away, turning my gaze up to the sky, burrowing further beneath the blanket even though I feel suddenly warm.

And as the night stretches on into hours of gentle bickering alternating with companionable silence, I let myself imagine that for the foreseeable future I'm not committed to living my astrological recommendations. That I also wasn't returning to my old life, the one where academic ambitions and relationships aren't compatible.

I let myself imagine who might be in that hypothetical, limitless, dream-world future.

The fact that Christian isn't the first person to pop to mind alarms me. Enough so that I make sure to call him and Kylee the moment I get back downstairs.

They're three hours behind, so I catch them just as they've finished up their pie.

"I miss you," Christian says after Kylee's wandered off to watch *Planes, Trains and Automobiles* with her grandparents.

"Me, too," I say. And I do mean it. I genuinely like Christian; I genuinely enjoy his company.

But as I drift off to sleep later that night, I can't help but wonder: Isn't there supposed to be . . . *more?*

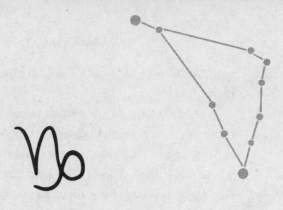

CAPRICORN SEASON

Buckle up, darling Gemini, because today's going to be a wild one. The Waxing Gibbous Moon in Aries combined with Mars in Libra square Pluto in Capricorn means the day is rife with high emotion and turmoil.

I go home to Boston for Christmas. I always go home to Boston for Christmas, and historically, I've always looked forward to it.

I feel lucky to have a family home to return to, one where not much has changed since I left. The Christmas tree is in the same corner it's always in. The angel at the top sits slightly crooked just as it did when I was little. My parents aren't the type to redo their kids' bedrooms after they've moved out. I'd like to think it's for nostalgic reasons, but I honestly think they just can't be bothered. As such, my childhood bedroom is more or less untouched from my teen years. There's still the periodic table of elements on the back of my bedroom door. The poster of the boy band hidden behind it. The deep purple bedding that I'd proudly replaced my little kid star sheets with. And books. A *lot* of books, all physics adjacent. Most of them gifts.

I've always found the return to this space comforting. A reminder that even though everything changes, some things stay the same. This year, however, the room feels stifling. The whole *house* feels stifling. The conversation most of all. Not that much has even been directed my way. From the moment I landed at Logan International Airport, I've felt like an obligation that nobody has the heart to ignore completely, but nobody wants to quite deal with, either.

As always, every family gathering has been a litany of various career achievements, discussions of the latest academic journals, and a surprising amount of scholarly gossip.

I used to love it.

Now I can't help but wonder: If I weren't present, would *I* be the gossip?

But it's Christmas. They're my family. And I love them.

So I've pasted on my smile. I've nodded along. I've made the requisite "I'm so impressed" noise at every last humble-brag.

And I've waited. For someone to ask about me. For a chance to tell them about Christian and Kylee. About how much I'm loving tutoring. About the Horoscope Project.

But by Christmas dinner, it's become painfully clear that the questions aren't coming. Now that I'm not playing their game, measuring myself by their same metrics, it's like I've been benched. Permitted to sit with the team, but not allowed on the field.

Over dessert—a mediocre, store-bought chocolate pie—I listen as they debate whose schedule is the most logical for taking me to the airport tomorrow morning, as though I'm a tedious but necessary errand. It's at that moment I decide . . .

I'm done with it.

"So, I'm a Gemini rising," I say, rather rudely interrupting.

The silence at the Reed family dinner table isn't quite deafening, but it's definitely present.

"I'm sorry." My father leans forward and cups his ear, as though his hearing is the issue. "What's this now?"

"You know. Astrology. As in you're a Virgo sun, like me, Dad."

"A Virgo . . . sun," he repeats. He looks completely confounded, which is an expression I've not ever seen on my brilliant father's face.

I glance around the table waiting for someone to ask about the distinction between sun sign and rising, what it means.

To ask anything at all. To *care*.

Instead, I get expressions that range from confusion on my brothers' faces to the pity on my mother's.

"Oh, Miranda," she says with a sigh. "I had no idea how much you were struggling."

"I'm not struggling, Mom. I'm . . . well, I kind of feel like I'm thriving, actually."

The second I say it, I realize how true it feels. Since my year of living by my horoscope is actually an academic year, I'm roughly halfway through. And though I'm still struggling to convince my brain that the moon appearing to be in front of Aries in the Northern Hemisphere on any given night could in *any* way determine how my day will go, I'm also realizing . . .

Maybe the whole point is that it has nothing to do with my brain. That it's the first time in my life where logic and facts haven't seemed quite as important as feeling . . .

Free.

"How can you be thriving?" my mom says fairly gently, but skeptically. "You're unemployed."

"I'm not . . ." I take a deep breath. "I'm choosing to explore a side of myself that's not just about logic and facts. I would love your support on this."

"But what happens after this . . . sabbatical?" my dad asks. "When you have to go back to real life?"

I literally bite my tongue to keep from retorting that my life right now isn't any less *real* just because it looks different from theirs. But if I'm being honest, I know the question is one I'll need to start dealing with. Lovely as these past few months have been, they're temporary.

Eventually the vacation will end, and I'll need to go back to work. To swallow my pride and go back to Nova as a lecturer. Or to try to find a new university to call home. But academia is a small world, and it'll have gotten out that I was denied tenure. Any university that looks at me will be looking at a reject.

A semi-famous reject, but still. I'm not exactly holding my breath for Columbia or Princeton to come calling.

"Yeah. You can't pretend to be a wizard forever, Miranda," my brother Jamie chimes in with a wink.

My other brother, Brian, nods, and from the serious set of his mouth, I can tell he agrees with Jamie.

"I'm still a scientist. And you know what?" I snap. "Even if I *weren't*, even if I didn't want to be a scientist, would I be a lesser person? Any less of a daughter or sister?"

I'm not exactly sure where all of this is coming from—it just sort of spills out. And then keeps spilling.

I shift all of my attention to my parents. "When did I want to become an astronomer?"

My mother looks startled. "I don't know, exactly. Weren't you nine or so?"

"And was that before or after you sent me to science camp?"

"You loved science camp!"

"Yes, but was it my *idea*?" I ask, because suddenly, I need to know.

Suddenly, it feels *vital* that I know.

To know whether this life I've been chasing, this aspiration of being a full professor, of dedicating myself to one university and one field of study for the rest of my life . . .

Is it *my* dream?

Or was it planted? Not with malicious intent, but simply because that's what Reeds do.

"Sweetheart." My dad's voice is uncharacteristically gentle. "You're brilliant. Whatever recent setbacks you've experienced, none of us have ever doubted that. We did our best to give you every opportunity. To foster that brilliance."

"I know, Dad," I say, setting my elbows on the table and rubbing my temples, suddenly exhausted. "I guess . . . I guess I just want to know if I'd still have a spot at this table if the IQ tests and my grades and my ambitions were different."

"Well, of course." My mother is affronted. "You're family."

The relief that I feel at this vanishes with her next words. "And *as* your family, we need to tell you that we're concerned. To your father's point, you're far too intelligent to be squandering your time with fantasy. A sabbatical, fine. But you're hurting your reputation, and ours with it."

There it is.

"Ah," I say, lightly. "So all of you are embarrassed by me."

I look around the table. My sister-in-law Emily, the only nonacademic, nonscientist at the table, who let me have her natal chart, gives me a small smile and shakes her head, but the rest of them avoid eye contact.

"You're just so high profile," my brother Jamie says a little guiltily. "Or you were. Everyone's wondering why you're no longer on the morning shows, and if *Jeopardy!* dropped you."

I shift uncomfortably, not wanting to admit even to myself how much it's been on my mind that those invitations have dried up entirely.

"Wait." I lift a hand, deflecting. "I thought you guys all hated that I did the public stuff."

"We did," Brian chimes in. "But now that you're not doing it, people want to know why."

"We just want to *understand*," my mother says, practically pleading. "And know what to tell people. About what your plan is."

"Tell them that I'm figuring out how to be happy," I say, pushing back from the table. "And that it's not happening at this dinner table."

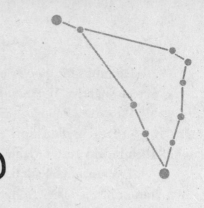

CAPRICORN SEASON

Today you'll find yourself pulled in a forbidden direction. Proceed with caution; something that feels seductive and irresistible today is unlikely to serve you well in the future. Prepare to feel a pull toward unfamiliar paths. Trust your instincts, but be ready to take a step back to reassess before committing further.

Y ou're sure this isn't some sort of terrible dating faux pas?" Christian asks, his smile just as cute on FaceTime as it is in person. "Are we at the point where I can ask you these sorts of painful favors?"

"It's a holiday party," I say, taking a sip of my tea. "That's not painful."

"It's a *work* holiday party. For someone else's work. The small talk required of you alone will likely be excruciating."

"Nah. The most uncomfortable part will be the high heels," I reply.

Well, and the strapless bra.

"If we were going to my work holiday party, I'd be dragging you," I add. "So consider us hypothetically even."

155

He props his elbows on his knees and leans toward the screen slightly. "You bummed?"

I frown. "About?"

"That they didn't invite you. Technically, you're still part of their faculty roster, right?"

"Technically," I admit. "And actually . . . I did get an invitation."

He blinks. "Yeah? Was it while you were in Boston?"

"Nope. It was the week before."

"And you didn't want to go?"

I snort. "Not even a little bit."

He smiles but looks a little bothered. "You don't think that'll come across as sour grapes, as my mom would say?"

"They already denied me tenure, Christian. And forced me into a sabbatical. I am feeling a bit sour toward them."

"As you should!" he agrees quickly. "I'm just looking forward to watching you get back on the top of your game. Making them see they screwed up."

I sip my tea again, a little surprised by the flicker of annoyance I feel at his words and the implication that being at the top of my game means reclaiming my place at Nova. And I suppose he's not wrong. That is where I'm likely headed back to, after all.

"I know you weren't up for going out tonight. But you're sure I can't bring you dinner?" he asks.

Christian had suggested we grab dinner and recap our respective holidays, but I'd requested a rain check. Hence the FaceTime. I got back home from Boston a few hours ago, and all I really want is a good night's sleep and some alone time.

"I'm good," I say. "Thanks, though. And I'll see you in a couple days for your party."

He touches his ear. "Ah. I'm hearing a dismissal."

"You're hearing the aftermath of a Reed family Christmas."

"Not a good visit?"

"Eh. You know how the holidays can be."

"I want to hear all about it. Later."

"Thanks," I say. "Tell Kylee I say hi."

Christian rolls his eyes. "I will if she ever comes out of her room."

"Good Christmas haul for her?"

"Let's just say her mom and I *may* have made a mistake by giving in to the video game console request. Now I have to go tell her she's reached her daily limit of screen time. Pray for me."

"Godspeed," I say with a laugh as I end the call.

I make myself another cup of tea, and then, because I'm tired but not quite sleepy, I grab my coat and watering can and make my way up to the roof. The forecast called for clouds all night, and there's only a crescent moon today, so I'm not expecting to see Archer, but the Buzzes still need their water. Sure enough, the roof is practically pitch-black as I make my way to the plants. A quick poke of the soil tells me Archer made good on his promise to water the plants while I was gone.

When I turn to go back inside, I let out a squeaking noise, because Archer is sitting at my outdoor table. Lounging, actually, legs outstretched, hands crossed over his thick winter jacket as he stares up at the cloudy sky.

"Hey! What are you doing over here?" There's no sign of his easel.

He looks my way. "Randy. Good Christmas?"

I let out a little huff and drop into the chair beside him.

"Same," he remarks.

"You stayed here, right?" I ask, since I haven't seen much of him the past few weeks. December weather doesn't exactly lend itself to lingering outdoors on the roof at night.

"Yup."

"Alone?"

He looks over. "I like being alone. But no. My brother and his family were here for a couple days."

"Oh. I don't think I knew you had a brother. Any nieces or nephews?"

"Three. All under the age of five. Hence this," he says, pointing at the generous whiskey jar in front of him.

Wordlessly, I reach out and help myself to a sip, then do a double take when I see a bulky object covered by a sheet beside the table and chairs. "What the heck is that?"

He shrugs. "Was here when I came up."

"And you didn't think to inspect it?"

"It's your roof, Randy."

"Right. Because you're *so* diligent about respecting my personal space," I reply, setting my mug on the table and reaching for the base of the sheet.

"I'd tug it carefully," Archer says, his tone a touch more hurried than usual. "Don't yank."

"Aha, so you *do* know what it is," I say, taking his advice and sliding the sheet off gingerly.

What's beneath leaves me speechless.

"It's a telescope," I say, running a hand reverently over the tube, casting a stunned glance over at Archer. "Is this . . . from you?"

He shrugs. "It was selfishly motivated. I figured it could be something to keep you busy while you're up here instead of talking at me."

158

I'm too flustered by the generous and thoughtful gift to come up with a retort, or to point out that he's the one on my roof.

As though he was waiting for me.

To give me the telescope. A telescope. A gift that's so thoughtful, so perfect, I can't even quite comprehend it.

He clears his throat. "Kylee mentioned you donated yours. Didn't seem right, you not having one."

I run a hand over it, dying to try it out, but I know from experience that I can lose myself for hours on the viewing end of a telescope, and I want to give him *his* gift.

"Don't move," I say, pointing at him. "I got something for you, too."

I race down the stairs to retrieve the present I'd gotten for Archer, suddenly giddy to have him open it.

The box is large and bulky, so I take my time carrying it back up the steps. I make a little sound of dismay when I see he's no longer sitting at the table, but then I see him on his own roof, heading back toward me.

"Here, wait. Stay there," I say, walking toward him. "This actually goes right where you're standing."

I start to step over the gap between our two roofs, but he makes a sharp warning noise. "Careful. It's icy."

Archer sets aside the blanket he must have retrieved while I was downstairs and takes the gift from me.

He surprises me then, setting the gift next to the blanket and extending a hand to me. I hesitate a moment before taking it. Rationally, I know he's just being a gentleman to keep me from slipping.

Emotionally, touching him seems . . .

Risky.

Finally, I place my hand in his. I don't mean to look at him. I don't want to look at him, but my gaze is pulled to his like a magnet.

Carefully, I step onto his roof, but not carefully enough, because my foot slips just a little. His other hand comes up to my back to steady me. "Okay?" he asks.

I let out a laugh that sounds a bit strained with embarrassment and . . . something.

"Yeah. I'm good."

His blue eyes hold mine for a moment longer before he nods and releases me.

He looks down at the gift. "You didn't have to get me anything."

I roll my eyes. "Don't be *that* guy. Just open it."

Archer sets the box on the ground, kneeling to unwrap it as I watch with my bottom lip between my teeth, suddenly self-conscious. The idea for Archer's gift had come to me on a whim a couple of weeks ago. I actually hadn't even known it existed, but was thrilled when a bit of googling helped me find exactly what I'd been envisioning.

Now, however, it seems . . .

Goofy.

Maybe even outright embarrassing.

But when he finishes tearing off the paper, he doesn't laugh.

In fact, he doesn't do or say anything at all. He just stares at the image and name printed on the side of the large box.

"It's a lamp," I explain nervously. "Made for the outdoors. It's meant to emulate the moonlight, and I thought maybe . . . I thought you could use it when there isn't enough actual light for you to draw."

"Damn," he says softly.

"Stupid?" I ask, shoving my hands into my parka pockets.

Archer sets a hand atop the box and glances up at me. "No. It's a good gift, Randy. Really good."

I exhale in relief.

He stands and shoves his own hands into his pockets. "Want to put our new gifts to use?" he asks.

There's a hopefulness in his voice that causes a strange ache in my chest.

"But, if it's too cold—"

"Not too cold," I interrupt in an excited rush, though suspicion nips at the back of my mind that my enthusiasm doesn't just stem from the telescope.

Archer nods toward his door. "I'll go grab my stuff." Then he points at my roof. "Do *not* slip and die getting back over there."

I give him a little salute and gingerly make my way over to my own roof, though the gap between the buildings isn't much of a threat to anything other than my ego if I were to slip.

Once I land safely, I settle behind the telescope, letting out a happy sigh of delight when I position it and get my first look. Being just across the river from Manhattan means the stargazing conditions are hardly ideal. Even with a body of water between me and the skyscrapers, their light pollution is still very present. But even that can't dampen the wonder of it.

Not too long later, I hear the bang of Archer's door as he comes back outside, followed by the sound of a box cutter and the rustle of packaging.

A long time later, I pull myself away from my new telescope and glance over to see him busily sketching away, his new moon lamp giving off a warm, soft glow beside him.

And then, even though it's late, I go back to stargazing, surprised to realize that my desire for an early bedtime and being alone don't seem to apply when I'm up here.

Mostly, I try very hard not to think about the reason. Or that the man beside me might be the very thing my horoscope was warning me about.

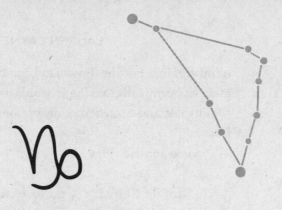

CAPRICORN SEASON

Today's energy will feel distinctly conflicted for you,
darling Gemini. A nagging awareness lies beneath
the surface. Resist the urge to dig too deep too fast.
The universe's timetable is not to be trifled with.

O h my god. Please no," I say, urgently pivoting away from
the mirror and craning my neck over my shoulder so I
can see my back in the reflection. "Oh, you have *got* to be kidding me."

I have less than an hour until Christian picks me up for his
company's holiday party, and in the process of trying on my
two dress options, I've managed to get the zipper of one stuck.

In my underwear.

It's one of those horrible women-living-alone moments that
I always knew I was overdue for, but the timing could not be
worse. If I were still in Manhattan, I was friendly enough with
the female professor next door to me in campus housing to ask
for the awkward favor, but here . . .

I try to tug at it but have no luck. The underwear I don't

163

mind ripping, but the dress had been blisteringly expensive, and I've been really looking forward to wearing it tonight.

I exhale and contemplate my options given how little time I have.

I come up with three.

1. Wait for Christian to get here, and embarrassingly ask him to free me.
2. Cancel.
3. It feels almost too unthinkable to name, and yet . . .

I pull on yoga pants under my skirt, fuzzy knee socks over the yoga pants, and then hurry downstairs to pull on my boots and parka. Opening the door, I shuffle down the pathway to my front gate, over to Archer's, and then toward his front door.

It's slow going, because New Jersey got its first sort-of snowfall last night. I say sort of because it was just a wet inch or two that has now turned mostly to slippery gray slush, but regardless, I really don't want to add a wet ass or broken wrist to the night's embarrassment.

"Please, please be home," I mutter as I impatiently push Archer's doorbell.

He opens it after a long while, his irritation turning to surprise when he sees me. "Randy. What are you doing here?"

"Oh, please. You come over to my house uninvited all the time," I say, pushing him aside so I can step into his foyer.

"You got this dolled up to come snoop on my studio?" he asks, shutting the door.

"For the hundredth time, I don't give a fig about your studio," I say. "You've made it abundantly clear that nobody's allowed in there."

"So you're here because . . ."

"I need a favor." I cross my arms. "And you have to promise not to laugh."

He shakes his head. "Absolutely not."

I sigh. "Fine. But I'm not going to ask this favor standing in your freezing cold entryway."

He nods toward the kitchen, and I follow him.

I've only been to Archer's house a handful of times, mostly to borrow a screwdriver because I still can't figure out where Lillian put hers, and once because I ran out of laundry detergent.

It's homier than one would expect from someone as gruff as Archer, but masculine, too. The layout is the same as mine, but instead of Lillian's floral wallpaper, Archer's walls are painted a dark gray, almost black. All of the color comes from the varied artwork on the walls.

"None of these are your pieces," I say, gesturing. I know next to nothing about art, but even though I've yet to see Archer's work in person, I know enough to recognize that these aren't his.

"Nope."

"Why not?"

"Because my art is my work. I keep my work in the studio, the same way other people leave their filing cabinet in their office."

I step into his kitchen, which is pleasingly modern. Lillian's appliances haven't been updated in years, and every surface is covered by a cookie jar or a collection of tea tins or a rooster made out of aqua blown glass. Archer's kitchen—again, despite having the same layout—looks nothing like this. The oven-and-stove combo is sleek with copper finish, and the only thing on the counters is a single whiskey bottle, which I now recognize as his beloved rye.

"What made you buy this place? Or rent?" I ask, looking over.

"Bought."

I'm dying to ask *how*, since he's barely older than me, and I know from Lillian that the row of cottages is both in demand and extremely expensive real estate. But the question is just a little too rude, even for Archer's particular blunt style of conversation.

"But you're an artist, and Manhattan is like . . . well, Daphne says it's an art-lovers mecca," I press.

"Art lovers, yes. Artists? I'm sure for some people the city serves as an inspiration. For me it feels more . . . like a distraction. I like being close enough that I can get to a gallery when I need to, but mostly I like the quiet and solitude. Or what used to be quiet and solitude," he adds, giving me a pointed look.

Feeling a little stung that he still feels that way, I look quickly away. I, too, felt like he'd intruded on my rooftop quiet and solitude the first day we'd met, but I haven't felt that way in . . . a while. I didn't realize he still did.

"Hey." Archer comes around the counter so he's on the same side as me. He leans back against it, crossing his arms and bending at the waist so his face is more at my level. "Randy."

"What."

He reaches out then, gently nudging my chin upward with the knuckle of is forefinger, though he drops it the second our eyes meet. "I didn't mean it like that."

"Uh-huh."

"I didn't. I mean . . ." He exhales, sounding frustrated.

166

"You did crash my solitude. But I don't . . . mind it. As much as I thought I'd mind it. Or at all, really."

"Oh. I—"

"What's your favor?" he interrupts.

"My favor . . . ohhhh. Oh yes," I say, remembering my dress. I point at his whiskey. "I'm going to need some of that."

He grabs the bottle and two mason jars—apparently, he doesn't own regular glasses—and pours us each a splash.

I toss mine back in a single swallow and his eyebrows go up. "How dire is this favor?"

"Dire," I say darkly. Before I lose my courage, I unzip my parka.

Archer's gaze follows the motion of the zipper, taking in the little black dress, which, from the front, is very conservative. From the back, too. When it's not gaping open.

"Please tell me you're not here for fashion advice. It looks fine."

"Thanks for the lavish praise, but no. I don't want your advice. I seem to be a little . . . stuck."

I turn around and, squinting my eyes shut as though I can block out the embarrassment, shrug my coat off.

There's a long moment of silence, and I brave a look over my shoulder to see Archer gazing at my exposed back, a hand covering the bottom half of his face.

"You said you wouldn't laugh," I accuse.

"No, I distinctly remember that I did not promise that," he says, dropping his hand and exposing his smile, which, while not an outright grin, is about as effusively amused as I've ever seen him.

"Just. Fix it. But please don't break the zipper. I'm rather attached to this dress."

167

He tosses back his drink, then steps toward me. His eyes meet mine for a split second before I whip my head back around.

"What are you all dressed up for anyway?" he asks.

I jump a little at the brush of his fingers on my lower back.

"Sorry." His voice is gruff. "My hands cold?"

Not even a little bit.

"No, it's fine." I clear my throat. "Um, Christian's company holiday party is tonight. He's picking me up in a bit, and I didn't want him to arrive finding me . . . like this."

"For what it's worth, I doubt he'd have minded," Archer says. "Typically men enjoy finding the women they're seeing in underwear. Particularly the black variety."

My cheeks heat in a flush, and I'm not sure if it's from embarrassment or proximity.

"How'd you even manage this anyway?" he mutters.

"My underwear is lace," I say defensively. "The fabric is prone to snagging."

"Yes, I see that," he says a bit under his breath.

A long minute later, he makes a gratified grunt, and the zipper glides upward.

"Thank you," I say with relief as he pulls the tab all the way to the top. "Would you mind . . . there's a little hook thing."

"Got it."

He fastens it and then steps back as I turn around.

"Well?" I spread my arms to the side, glancing down. The dress was rather demure on the hanger. Perhaps demure now, too, but I rather like the way it's formfitting enough to look feminine but not so tight as to remove all mystery.

"Nice socks," he said, jerking his chin toward the fuzzy purple socks I'd pulled on for warmth.

I drop my arms, a little deflated, though I don't know what

I was expecting since he's already declared the dress an underwhelming *fine*.

"Thanks for your help," I say, meaning it. "I promise I won't make a habit of it."

"I mean, anytime you want to trot over here in black lace panties . . ." His smile is quick, just a flash of teeth.

"Yes, right. Because you seem very overcome by my feminine wiles," I say just a bit waspishly as I march back toward his front door, pulling my jacket back on as I move.

Archer follows me out to the foyer, though when I open the front door, he places his palm on it to close it again.

I glance up in question, and his blue eyes are guarded as he briefly clenches his jaw. "Hey. Randy. You look . . . nice. Okay? You look good."

The guarded gaze drops for a split second, revealing what I could have sworn is a flash of heat before it disappears.

"Better," I say, trying for levity but sounding breathy.

As far as compliments go, Archer's words aren't exactly poetry. So I can't explain why my body feels distinctly overheated on the walk back to my house despite the subfreezing temps.

Or why, hours later, even as I'm in Christian's arms, I swear I can still feel the brush of Archer's fingers on my lower back . . .

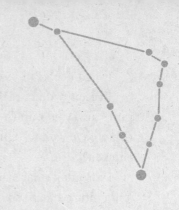

♑

CAPRICORN SEASON

*Fireworks will send you careening in an exhilarating
new direction, darling Gemini. Lean into what scares
you, as your greatest adventure begins with a leap
into the unknown. The universe is aligning to guide
you, so embrace the fireworks and let them light up
your path to new horizons.*

A fireworks prediction on New Year's Eve? Color me unim-
pressed with Zodiac Zone's on-the-nose horoscope today.
I don't *love* this holiday. Never have.

Most years, I spend New Year's Eve in sweatpants on my
couch, in bed by ten, and honestly? I've always been perfectly
content with that tradition.

However, apparently that was how Dr. Miranda Reed, PhD,
spent New Year's Eve. Miranda, the budding astrologist?

She apparently has *plans*.

Last-minute invitations, *two* of them, that my December 29
horoscope had strongly suggested I accept.

The evening started in Manhattan. Christian made reser-
vations at a fancy jazz supper club on the Upper West Side.

171

It had been fun. Okay, it had been *fine*.

I actually don't really love the prix fixe menus that restaurants always do on these kinds of holidays. Why does everything have to have truffles? What if I just want the freaking chicken?

I also don't particularly love jazz. I know that it's trendy and cultured to do so, but I just . . . don't. It's too chaotic.

And last, and this one's a real kicker.

I don't love the man.

I don't think I'm ever going to love the man.

I *like* Christian. A lot. But it's getting harder and harder to avoid the truth:

Written in the stars or not, Christian Hughes is not the guy for me. It's why I'm never in a hurry to return his calls or texts. It's why I can never quite relax around him.

It's why I'd been secretly relieved when he'd told me that he won't be able to stay over tonight after all because her mother had needed to swap her Kylee days, and Kylee would be dropped off early at his house tomorrow.

Tonight was supposed to be *the* night with Christian, but I know in my gut that this isn't merely a reprieve or delay. It's a sign.

If it weren't for Kylee getting more attached, I might try a bit longer, but I won't risk breaking that little girl's heart when things inevitably fall apart with her father. Not even for the sake of the Horoscope Project.

But that's January's problem.

My genius may not always extend to my skills in the relationship department, but even I know not to break up with someone on New Year's Eve, especially when we have another party to go to.

Archer's party.

I didn't even know those two words could go together, but the invitation had come through a couple of days ago.

And actually, *invitation* is a bit of a euphemism for "terse command delivered via text."

NYE party at my place. Alyssa's hosting and told me to include you. Come.

Alyssa.

The woman whom, until just recently, I thought he might have made up.

Whom maybe a tiny part of me *wishes* he'd made up. A part of me that, per my horoscope, I am determined not to indulge.

I haven't been particularly excited about a party with a bunch of people I don't know, so it feels like a bit of a blessing that it's already past eleven by the time we get home from the city. That means I'll have to endure less than an hour of small talk before the countdown. With any luck, I'll be able to make my date with my trusty Waterpik by twelve fifteen.

"So, tell me about this Alyssa," Christian says as we pull on our coats to make the short but freezing walk to Archer's. "Anything I need to know?"

"I haven't met her, actually. All I know is that she's some sort of hotshot agent. Archer says she specializes in celebrities who pivot from one career to another. Athletes who become sportscasters, singers who become talk show hosts, actresses who want to do food shows. That kind of thing."

"Interesting. How'd she and Archer meet?"

"Well, the details are scant, because Archer's conversational skills are scant, but I believe some sort of reality show was looking to do an artist-in-residency thing. They wanted Archer to get involved. Then she got involved. Then she and Archer got involved."

"They must be *very* involved if they're throwing a party together."

"Um, I think *together* might be a misnomer," I say. "Archer's not really the party type. I got the feeling this was Alyssa's idea."

"Think she invited us so you won't call the cops if they get loud?"

"Eh. I'm thinking it's more likely she wants access to my roof."

"Your roof? It's not even thirty degrees tonight."

"Lillian says you can see the midnight fireworks from up there. Maybe their guest list is too big to fit onto just Archer's roof?"

I don't tell him how much the thought of anyone being on my roof bothers me.

I'm possessive of my roof.

Only my roof. Definitely only possessive of the roof.

When we get next door, there's a note on Archer's door telling people to come on in. The wave of noise that hits us when I push it open tells me that this is not the small get-together I'd been hoping for.

"Hi! Come on in," a tall blonde says when we step into Archer's kitchen. "You must be the neighbor and neighbor's boyfriend. Welcome! I'm Alyssa."

"Hi, I'm Miranda. This is Christian."

Alyssa, as I had prepared for, is gorgeous. She's also a bit older than I'd have thought. Older, I think, than Archer by a few years—though there's nothing about her that comes across as *old*, just . . . interesting, as though she has a million stories to tell, and all of them would be as sparkly and light as she is.

Because *damn it*. She seems really likable.

"I'm so glad you could make it," she says, ushering us further into the space. "Here! Champagne."

She grabs two crystal flutes that must be rented, because I can't imagine Archer owning anything so fussy, and points us toward an ice bucket where several champagne bottles are already open.

"That's Jackson Burke," Christian murmurs in my ear as he pours us each a glass. The name doesn't mean anything to me, but his excitement is plain as he looks across the room to a tall, handsome man with his arm around a pretty blonde.

"Who?" I accept the champagne, trying not to think about how wrong it feels that it's not a mason jar with Michter's rye. Trying not to feel like all of these people in Archer's place feels wrong.

"Former quarterback and the Super Bowl rings to prove he was a good one," Alyssa explains, having overheard Christian's and my conversation. "Client of mine."

She grins at Christian. "You want an introduction?"

"Oh man." Christian is a little starstruck, and it's kind of adorable. "Hell yes."

I touch his arm. "You go. I'm going to run to the restroom."

Alyssa points. "First door on left."

I suck in my cheeks to keep from saying that I know where the bathroom is. That I've been here before. Not often, but more often than *she* has, at least recently.

I shake my head to clear it. *What is wrong with you, Miranda? The house isn't yours. Neither is the man . . .*

I don't actually need to use the restroom. I do need just a

moment to retreat and center myself. I've never enjoyed high-energy gatherings, and with this one coming on the heels of Christian's holiday party a couple of days earlier, my supply of small talk topics is feeling a bit exhausted.

The bathroom is occupied when I get there, so I hover in the hallway, taking in the various art pieces. They're different from the ones in Archer's entryway. Sketches, mostly, but they're all framed. To my untrained eye, it seems like an eclectic collection, no two pieces by the same artist, and not a single one signed by Archer himself.

I get to the end of the hallway, where, in my home, Lillian's bedroom is located. It's not the largest bedroom in the home, but she'd moved to it following her hip surgery a couple of years ago to minimize the use of stairs.

The equivalent door in Archer's home is shut, and taped to it is a handwritten sign with the words *Keep Out* underlined for emphasis.

The note on the front door tonight, inviting people inside, had been written in a pretty feminine script, probably by Alyssa.

There is nothing pretty about this assertive, terse scrawl.

This is Archer's studio.

"Well, well. The white whale," I murmur, because anytime I've even looked at his house, he's made a point of telling me that no one is allowed inside the studio. Ever.

I lift a hand to the doorknob, then swiftly snatch it back.

What am I doing?

I am a rule follower. I respect other people's personal space.

I would never jeopardize Archer's trust.

And yet . . .

The sudden urge to know a little bit more about the man feels impossible to resist.

I bite the corner of my lip, hesitating only a moment longer before glancing over my shoulder for witnesses, and then slip into the off-limits room.

Even if I didn't know it was Archer's studio, the smell would be a dead giveaway: paint mixed with Archer's soap or cologne, or whatever makes him smell like . . . him.

For some reason I was picturing white. White walls, maybe a white painter's tarp on the floor to catch any messes. But aside from a stack of white canvases stacked neatly in a corner, everything else is darkly masculine. The floors are dark hardwood. Clean, but not polished. There's a large storage cabinet on the far wall, but the rest of the brick walls are covered, as I suppose one would expect, with art. Archer's art.

This same room in Lillian's *should* feel the same, and I suppose there are similarities, but somehow this feels fundamentally Archer.

The space is lit by a warm glow, and I smile to realize it's the moon lamp I got him for Christmas. He's moved it in for the party. Logically, I know it was to make more room on the roof for watching the fireworks at midnight, but I like the idea that he put it in here so nothing would happen to it.

I pivot toward what must be his workstation, an enormous wooden table covered in paint and a no-nonsense wooden stool tucked into the shadows, with . . .

A man sitting on it.

I jump so hard some of my champagne sloshes onto my hand. I shake it off. "Damn it, Archer. What are you doing in here?"

He, too, is holding a flute of champagne, and he takes a small sip before speaking. "Now. Which one of us should be asking that question?"

I flinch because I know he's exactly right. I'm the one who shouldn't be in here, and entering without permission was actually a really crappy thing to do. "I'm so sorry. I'm *really* sorry. And I'm leaving," I say, backing up slowly. "And sorry again."

"Randy."

"Yeah?" I brace for a well-deserved rebuke for my intrusion.

He sighs. "First the roof, now my studio. I must be getting used to your presence, because somehow, I'm not mad."

I narrow my eyes suspiciously at his champagne flute. "Uh-huh. Exactly how many of those have you had?"

He waggles it. "First glass. Not really a champagne guy."

Shocker. I study him. "You're really not upset?"

He shakes his head.

I ease slightly closer. "Why are you in here? You're hosting a party."

"No." He sips more champagne. "Alyssa is hosting a party. At my house. I don't know half the guest list."

"I thought she has a place in the city."

"She does. Tribeca. But no outdoor space, so no view of the"—he motions upward with a disinterested wave—"fireworks."

"Ah. That makes sense. She's very pretty," I say as I begin to wander around the studio. Whether he's accustomed to me or not, I don't anticipate another chance to be in here.

"Yes."

"These are bigger than they look online," I say, stopping in front of a large canvas that is taller than I am, and apparently his work in progress.

I tilt my head, recognizing the distinct pyramid shape in the foreground instantly. "Paris. This your next series? Daphne's been wondering."

He looks startled. And annoyed. "You talk to Daphne about my art?"

"Nope. *She* talks to *me* about it. She's a huge art buff. Apparently, everyone is speculating over your next move."

"Fantastic," he mutters.

"Is this where you were when I first moved in here?" I ask, looking back at the canvas. "Paris?"

He nods. "Three months."

"Three months!" I say in surprise.

"That's how long it took to get a feel for the tone I wanted. I was in Tokyo for six months for the first series."

"You always do cities? Travel focused?"

"No. The Tokyo one was unplanned. I went to visit a friend for a week. Felt inspired. Stayed. Painted."

"Daphne told me it made a huge splash in the art world. That you'd been popular, but this bumped you up to the next level."

He stands, joining me in front of the canvas to stare down at it. "People like the travel pieces, I guess."

"Probably because it presents an escape from their current world. Especially when it's this large, this vibrant. You must *feel* that when you paint them."

"Sometimes."

I look over. "You don't sound particularly . . . enraptured."

He shrugs. "Escaping from your current reality is only desirable when you don't *like* your current reality. Tokyo was great, because at the time I was feeling . . . lost."

It's about as emotional an admission as I've ever heard from Archer, and even though I'm dying to know if it has to do with his failed engagement, I also know to tread carefully. If I don't ease open this door into his soul very gently, he'll slam it shut again.

179

In fact, instinct tells me to say nothing. To wait.

After a moment, my instincts are rewarded. "I went there after Willow . . . ended things." He gives me a wry look. "But you already knew that."

I shake my head. "All the internet knows is that you two were engaged and that it ended. Not that *she* ended it. Or why."

Or that you felt lost afterward.

The very mental image makes me feel like crying.

"I'm not even sure I know why it ended," he says with a harsh laugh that does little to mask the pain in his voice.

"She didn't tell you?"

"Oh, she told me," he says, still staring at the Paris painting, though I don't think he's really seeing it. "Her *psychic* told her we weren't a match."

My mouth drops a little. "Her . . . psychic."

"Well, Willow called him a *spiritual adviser*. Whatever you call the bastard, he informed her that the stars or the universe or whatever the hell didn't want us to be together. It was nine days before the wedding."

I set my hand on his arm. "Archer. That's . . . I don't even know what that is. Horrible."

Heartbreaking.

He looks down. "Maybe it ended for the best. Forced me to set up some new rules, and I'm better for it."

"What rules?"

Archer's head tips back and he drains the last of his champagne in a single gulp. "No dating anyone who would put the *universe's* wishes above her own."

Before I can properly process that, I hear a loud murmur of voices from the other side of the door, followed by the clomping of footsteps.

I look upward. "Must be coming up on midnight. Everyone's headed up for the countdown."

He glances at his watch. "Nine minutes."

I nod, fully intending to join the group. To join Christian. But my feet don't move.

Archer must feel the same, because instead of suggesting we go see the fireworks, he gestures with his empty glass at the Paris piece in front of us. "What do you think of this, Randy?"

I shift my attention to the art, startled by the subject change, but also sensing he *needs* the subject change.

"I think it's beautiful," I say honestly. He's painted the famous pyramid in front of the Louvre, but he's taken liberties with colors and perspective. There are none of the soft colors and delicate silhouettes that one associates with Paris. It looks like an alternate-universe version, one that begs to be explored.

He nods. "Yeah. It is."

I look up at his tense profile. "You don't sound happy."

"I don't know," he says, sounding frustrated. "The Paris series isn't consuming me the way that I'd hoped."

"That's how you want to feel? Consumed?"

"When it comes to my art, yes. Otherwise, what's the point?"

"Hmm." I scratch my cheek. "Well. Is there anything that *does* consume you lately? Perhaps that's what you're meant to work on."

"Yes." He's distracted. "But it's nothing like my Tokyo series. And that's what people want. Expect."

I smile. "Take it from someone who abandoned the world of logic and science to detour to astrology. Sometimes eschewing expectations opens unexpected doors."

He doesn't smile back. "Unexpected doors. Like the one that led you to Christian."

I hesitate.

Now doesn't seem the moment to explain that I plan to end things with Christian. Or maybe it's *exactly* the moment, and that terrifies me, because I say nothing.

Archer turns to face me, giving me a slow once-over. "Same dress as the other night."

I glance down. "It makes the rounds during the holiday season."

"Same undergarments as well?"

My brain scrambles for a witty retort, something to ease the tension, but the memory of his fingers on my skin when he'd zipped my dress the other night, when he'd *seen* said underwear, seems to overwhelm my every thought, and all I manage is a nod.

Neither of us says anything for a long moment. The silence isn't uncomfortable, but there's a new tension that seems to crackle between us.

It's broken only by a series of sharp popping noises, so unexpected that I jump, putting a hand over my heart, which is racing for *two* reasons now.

"Fireworks," Archer says a bit tersely, not breaking eye contact.

I swallow. "It must be midnight. Should we . . . sing 'Auld Lang Syne,' or something?"

His mouth twitches in the corner, his gaze flashing with something that is probably amusement, but for a moment looks an awful lot like affection.

"Come on, Randy," he says softly, taking the glass from my hand and setting it aside with his own. "That's no way to ring in the New Year."

Before I can register his meaning, he lowers his face to

mine. He pauses a heartbeat before the kiss, his eyes holding my own, burning with an emotion I don't recognize.

Archer's lips brush over mine.

And every cell in my body seems to wake up from a life-long sleep.

Objectively, it resembles a standard-issue New Year's Eve kiss. A friendly peck much like the ones being exchanged all over the eastern time zone right now. Like the meaningless kisses likely being exchanged on our own roof this very moment.

Subjectively?

There is nothing standard about the kiss.

Not the way his lips linger a moment longer than they should.

Not the way it robs me of my breath.

Or the way I *ache* with the urge to pull him back. To kiss him again. To never stop.

Slowly I force my eyes open, finding Archer's face still mere inches from my own, his dark blue gaze reflecting my same frustrated want back to me.

"Happy New Year, Randy," he says, his voice a gruff whisper.

"Happy New Year," I whisper back. My gaze drops back to his mouth.

Lean into what scares you, as your greatest adventure begins with a leap into the unknown . . .

This. *This* is what scares me. Because whatever it is feels too *big* to fit into the temporariness of what this experimental, sabbatical year is supposed to be.

Lean into what scares you . . .

Lifting to my toes, I press my mouth to his.

Archer's response is immediate, as though he's been waiting for this moment. *Wanting* it.

His other hand comes up so he's cupping my face, fingers sliding into my hair as he tilts my head and deepens the kiss. His lips nudge mine apart, hungry and purposeful. My tongue shyly touches his and he lets out a masculine, gratified groan that I feel down to my very core.

My hands have been resting lightly on his chest, but now my fingers dig into the soft cashmere of his sweater, pulling him closer, needing more . . .

Somewhere, a door slams, followed by the sound of laughing voices coming back down the stairs.

The reality of what I'm doing sinks in and I pull my lips from his with a gasp.

Archer and I stare at each other, breathing hard, the space between us charged with uncertainty and something I don't know how to name.

I lift a trembling hand to my lips. "Archer . . ."

His gaze is searching mine, looking for something. "Did that have anything to do with your horoscope?"

I'm still feeling off-balance, so it takes me a second to register his question. "What?"

His fingers, still in my hair, tighten slightly. "Your horoscope, Randy. Did that have anything to do with what just happened?"

"I . . ." Still trying to sort my thoughts. "Well, yes, but—"

He releases me abruptly, pivoting away from me, digging his fingers into his own hair this time. "*Damn* it, Randy!"

Startled and confused by his vehemence, I shake my head. "I don't understand, what—"

He turns back toward me, his expression closed off and unreadable. "You should go find Christian," he says in a cold tone I've never heard before.

Christian. Guilt flares.

"Don't," Archer snaps, seeing my expression. "Don't feel guilty. It was just an inconsequential New Year's Eve kiss. That's all this was. He was doing the same thing upstairs. It didn't mean anything."

I swallow, but my feet don't move.

"You hearing me, Randy?" Archer says, his voice still cold, a little impatient now. "It didn't mean anything."

Finally, I snap out of my daze enough to know that I need to protect myself now. Before he can hurt me any further. "Yes, Archer. I have a 170 IQ. I think I can grasp a blatant rejection."

His jaw tenses, and for a moment I think—hope—he might contradict me, but instead he just gives a single nod.

I exit his studio, chin held high, but the second I slam the door behind me, I drop my chin to my chest, leaning against the wall for support.

My horoscope had been right about the fireworks, and they hadn't just been in the sky.

But it had also been damn wrong. Those fireworks sure as hell aren't lighting up my path to new horizons.

In fact, it feels very much like the end of something. Something that never had a chance to even start.

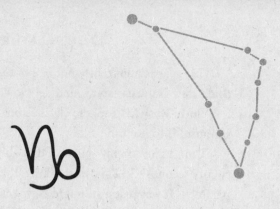

♑

CAPRICORN SEASON

*Today brings forward a pivotal decision that
demands both courage and self-awareness.
A second opinion will be helpful, but ultimately,
you'll need to trust your own instincts.*

The next afternoon, I'm at Daphne's apartment in Murray Hill for our long-standing tradition of New Year's Day chili and a *Friends* marathon.

Only this time, our favorite sitcom is a mere backdrop to the topic at hand:

The Kiss.

"Okay, so how long would you say the kiss lasted?" Daphne asks as she tops her chili with a very generous handful of cheddar cheese.

"The first or the second?" I ask, adding a scoop of sour cream to my bowl. The chili is actually Daphne's family's tradition, started by her grandfather. But every January 1, every member of the Cabbot family follows the same secret family recipe, though Daphne has been known to omit the meat from hers when she's on a vegetarian kick.

This year is apparently not one of those kicks, because the thick stew is meaty, spicy, and delicious.

"Both. Both kisses," she clarifies before shoving a generous spoonful into her mouth.

"Um." I blow on my spoon. "I'd say like, two seconds and . . . twenty seconds? So I'm overthinking it, right?" I ask a little desperately. "It was just a standard New Year's kiss?"

"Could have been," she admits. "I've had kisses with strangers on New Year's Eve that lasted longer than that, and one memorable kiss a few years ago with a bit of tongue." She pauses, reminiscing. "That was *hot*. Still regretting not getting his number." She shakes her head. "But back to last night . . . I don't think the duration of the kiss is the most pertinent factor here. It was the quantity. One kiss at midnight is simply tradition. Two is . . ."

"Is what?" I ask, when she pauses, trying and failing to keep the desperation out of my voice.

Instead of answering, she takes a sip of diet soda, and narrows her eyes slightly. "Did you tell Christian?"

I groan at the mention of his name. "No. He was all giddy from champagne and meeting his football idol and some actress whose name I've already forgotten. Apparently they shared a midnight smooch that would have blown teenage Christian's head clean off."

That last bit had gone a long way to make me feel better. Not all the way better, but . . . a little less guilty.

"So you two didn't . . . after?" Daphne makes a childish gesture with her hands.

I shake my head. "He took an Uber home after the party as planned."

But I had not gone to sleep immediately after. I'd spent

half the night tossing and turning, replaying the feel of Archer's mouth on mine. The other half of the night had been spent trying to block out the hurt that it had apparently meant nothing.

He could not have been more clear about that.

"Christian didn't notice you were gone at midnight?"

"He did, but he didn't seem to mind," I admit. "Like I said, the champagne was flowing, and he was starstruck by the guest list."

"See, so maybe the whole thing is nothing to stress about. New Year's Eve is just one of those weird little hall pass moments. And it only happens once a year. Didn't mean a thing."

I give a distracted nod.

"Wait." Daphne studies my face very carefully. "Did you *want* the kiss to mean something?"

"No," I answer quickly. "Why, do you think it did?"

"Sweetie, it's not what I think about last night. It's what *you* think. You were there. Feeling the feelings."

"But I'm bad at this stuff."

"What *stuff*?" she says, adding more cheese to her bowl.

"Understanding men. Understanding . . . moments."

"So it *was* a moment?" She watches me carefully.

"It sure felt like . . . something," I say, staring down at my chili. "But you should have seen his face when he told me to go find Christian. *Ordered* me to, really. It was like he thought he'd made a fatal error and was desperate to strike it from the record."

"Hmm." Daphne chews, looking thoughtful. "So what are you going to do?"

I push my chili around in my bowl. "I'm going to give Archer exactly what he wants and pretend it never happened."

Daphne sets her bowl aside and exhales. "Okay, I can't even believe I'm throwing this out there, but . . . you're not shutting out Archer because of astrological incompatibility, right?"

"Complete incompatibility," I say. "Literally everything about our charts points to disaster."

Based on last night, I'd have to say the stars had gotten it right here.

My best friend's eyes narrow ever so slightly. "And you're *sure* that's not just an excuse? Something to hide behind so you don't have to face pesky feelings."

I take a huge bite of chili so I don't have to acknowledge this. Aloud or in my own thoughts.

Daphne sighs. "I know that face."

"What face?"

"Your stubborn one. The expression you get when you're determined to use your head and *only* your head because it's easier."

"Easier than what?"

She gives me a patient look. "Listening to your heart."

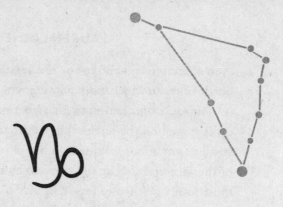

♑

CAPRICORN SEASON

Today, Gemini, an appealing opportunity comes knocking at your door. On the surface, it seems like a perfect fit. However, as Neptune squares Mars, you may find yourself grappling with a foggy sense of direction and conflicting impulses. This transit can bring confusion and misdirection. Keep all doors open, but don't walk through any quite yet.

Thanks for having me over. Especially after the debacle that was Christmas," my brother Jamie says as he nods in thanks for the glass of wine I hand him.

I wince and settle onto the couch, pulling my feet beneath me. "It wasn't a *debacle*." I sip my own wine. "Was it?"

"Emily's been calling it a *scene*, if you prefer that descriptor," Jamie says with a grin. "And if it makes you feel better, she thinks the show was fantastic. She's still talking about it. We all are."

"Oh wow, yeah. I feel *much* better now," I mutter.

My brother is in town for a conference and asked if we could have drinks before his dinner with his colleagues. He'd even offered to come to me on the Jersey side with a very nice bottle of wine, which we're now enjoying in the Cottage.

Jamie isn't bothering to hide his fascination with the colorful assault on the senses that is Lillian's living room, which still has our aunt's unique stamp and style all over it in spite of the fact that I've finally come to think of it first and foremost as my place, and less "Lillian's place." I've streamlined the kitchen, put unnecessary side tables in storage, and given just about every closet and bookshelf a thorough purge of stuff, all with Lillian's blessing.

But Lillian's unique presence is the strongest in this particular room, and it hadn't felt right to intrude upon it. It feels important, somehow, that I leave it alone. Mostly, it's just out of respect.

Though if I'm being really honest? That's only a partial truth.

Yes, with its loud, old-fashioned wallpaper, brightly colored, mismatched area rugs, and framed photos of, well, women's butts—though, to Lillian's point, *artsy* butts—the room is indeed as unique and nuanced as a fingerprint. *Lillian's* fingerprint.

So while my aunt had permitted me to put her stuff in storage—*encouraged* it, even—the truth is that I've left Lillian's living room exactly as is because I need the reminder.

A reminder that this isn't my home.

That this isn't my *life*.

I'm not *really* the person who picked up Ethiopian takeout for dinner last night because my horoscope suggested I try a new cuisine. I am not the person who is currently wearing a dark red lipstick because yesterday's horoscope advised Gemini to change up her look.

I like *pretending* to be that person. But in the New Year,

it's time to start preparing for reentry to real life. Because in just a few short months, I go back to being me. The real me. And I can't get too comfortable in someone else's home living someone else's life.

"I'd forgotten how weird Aunt Lillian is," Jamie says with a fond smile, picking up the small deck of cards on an end table. "These playing cards are creepy as hell."

"That's because they're not playing cards. They're tarot cards. And they're a collector's item, so put them back."

"Yes, *Mom*." Jamie obeys and lifts his hands in apologetic surrender before picking up his wineglass from the table and settling into a neon-green chair across from me.

He takes a sip and gives me a studying look. "So. How you doing?"

"Nope," I say immediately, shaking my head. "We're not doing that."

He looks confused. "Doing what? Caring about how my sister is doing?"

"I know that you care," I say, softening my tone. "I love that you care. But I'm so over the narrative of 'Poor Miranda is having a complete breakdown in the aftermath of getting denied tenure.' I'm fine. I'm more than fine."

He leans forward, his expression earnest. "Okay, but can I just plant this seed? A couple years ago, you were on that talk show. I'm forgetting which one. And the host specifically asked you about astrology. Do you remember that?"

I tense slightly because I know where this is going. "Of course I remember it, J. I was there."

"So you remember what you said?"

"I gently explained that there was no scientific evidence that cosmic events directly impact earthly events."

"Do you still stand by that assessment?" Jamie asks.

I lean forward and grab a couple of almonds off the charcuterie board I'd quickly put together. "I do."

My brother looks relieved, but my next words erase all of that.

"But I'm no longer sure that everything about the human experience can be explained by science. Or *should* be defined by science."

He exhales and sits back in his chair. "Damn. Aunt Lillian really has rubbed off on you."

"Have you ever read your horoscope?" I ask. "Read your natal chart? Studied Emily's chart in conjunction with yours? Wondered if the fact that your moon is in Cancer is the very reason you're here right now? Because nurturing family is important to you?"

My brother stares at me. "Of course not."

"Of course not," I repeat. "And yet you can sit there and tell me astrology isn't real. That what I've been doing these past few months is nonsense. You feel good about that, as a scientist? To form a conclusion without a *single* bit of data?"

Jamie closes his eyes for a moment, frustrated. "I didn't come here to fight."

"Why *did* you come here?" I ask, though I try to keep my voice gentle. "Did the parents send you to see if I'm still mad about Christmas dinner?"

He smiles a little. "I think they're still recovering from your accusation that they pushed you into science."

"I didn't mean it to be an accusation," I say, feeling guilty. "I just . . . wondered. Lillian implied there was a time when I wasn't quite so . . . logical. And lately I've been pondering if maybe she's right."

Jamie's smile widens. "Well, I do seem to remember one particular Christmas morning when Mom and Dad kept nudging you toward your new kiddie chemistry set, but you were *way* more into some stuffed pink pony with wings that Grandma Anne gave you. You 'flew' that thing everywhere."

I blink a little in surprise. "I don't remember that at all."

He shrugs. "You were like five. You grew out of it."

Did I?

A little part of me wonders if the girl who believed pink ponies could fly is still in there somewhere. If she didn't make an appearance that night at summer camp when she wished on a star. And if she's not showing herself now—in a woman who's letting herself believe, at least for a little while, that the universe has a plan for her, that the planets' transits can guide her days, and that the stars can lead her to love.

"Okay, confession time," Jamie says, setting his glass on a sparkly coaster. "I didn't just come here to catch up over wine. Or to check on you," he adds quickly. "I have an . . . opportunity to discuss."

"An opportunity for . . ."

"So, you remember Dr. Lisa Kelling?" he asks.

I scrunch my nose, trying to remember. "Is that the same Lisa you dated the year before you met Em? Few years older than you? Dry sense of humor?"

He nods.

"She was great. Why'd you break up again?"

"The long distance was wearing on us. She's at Stanford."

"Oh, that's right."

"Stanford's Physics Department," Jamie clarifies.

Ah.

"That's great for her," I say, then point at his glass to distract him. "More wine?"

I stand before he can reply, but Jamie refuses to let me back out of the conversation. He stands as well. "She called the other day. Managed about fifteen seconds of small talk before she got down to the real reason she was calling. You."

I don't want to be intrigued, but still . . .

Stanford.

"What about me?" I ask warily.

"She was feeling me out on your next steps."

I grunt. "So word about my tenure fail's officially out, huh?"

He gives an apologetic smile. "Sorry. You know how small the academic world can be."

"Small-minded," I mutter.

He shrugs. "Anyway. The head of her department wants to talk to you."

"Oh. Well. I'm flattered, but I have a job waiting for me at Nova."

"A school where you'll have to settle for *lecturer*," Jamie says.

"I'll have to settle for lecturer pretty much everywhere now," I say. "I'm damaged goods."

He shakes his head. "Not at Stanford. They're talking *tenure track*, Miranda."

I go still, not quite believing what I'm hearing. It's not completely unheard-of—though unlikely—that someone can get back on tenure track elsewhere after being denied, but never have I heard about someone getting a second chance at a place as prestigious as Stanford.

"You're kidding."

He shrugs. "Apparently some universities see your high profile as a boon. That, and you're brilliant," he adds quickly.

"Good save," is about all I can manage as my head swarms with possibilities and confusion.

Before I can even begin to sort through the conflicting thoughts, I hear the front door open.

"Randy? You home?"

Archer starts to pass through the open doorway, then pauses when he sees me in the living room.

His gaze finds mine over Jamie's shoulder, and this time, our gazes get tangled up, a million unidentifiable undercurrents passing between us.

It's the first time we've seen each other since New Year's Eve.

I've been telling myself that the winter weather is why I've dragged the Buzzes off the roof and into the greenhouse to protect the flowers from elements. I've been telling myself that Archer's deep into his Paris series, which is why he hasn't been over for leftovers.

But as his eyes meet mine now, I realize that those are all half-truths and excuses.

I've been avoiding him.

And I can see by the slight wariness in his eyes that he's been avoiding me, too.

He glances at my brother, who is already walking toward him to shake his hand.

"Hi, I'm Jamie. Miranda's brother. You must be Christian."

I let out a snort, and Archer's eyes narrow and land very briefly on me before he looks back to my brother. "Nope. Just the neighbor. Not the boyfriend."

Gosh, thanks for clarifying that, Archer. I wasn't sure where you stood on that front.

Technically, Christian is still my boyfriend. I'm still planning to break up with him as soon as possible, but he'd gotten a call on New Year's Day that he'd need to fill in for his boss at some big convention in Dallas, so he's been gone for a week. He's too good a guy to break up with over the phone or by text, so I'm waiting for him to get back to have the conversation in person.

"Oh, well. Good to meet you," Jamie says to Archer, seemingly oblivious to the tension in the room. If he thinks it's odd that my neighbor enters the house uninvited, he doesn't show it.

My brother glances at his watch and winces. "I've gotta run to this boring dinner at some boring steak house in midtown." He turns toward me. "You'll think about it."

I nod.

"*Really* think about it," he says, approaching me for a quick farewell hug. "And in return, I won't tell the parents about the offer. Yet."

I hug him back. "I promise."

He steps back and takes my shoulders for a second. "You deserve it, Miranda. It's the best thing."

Best thing for whom?

"I promise I'll give it serious consideration," I tell my brother. "Now *go*. It's rush hour; you're going to be late if you don't leave now."

He gives me a little salute, and with a nod of farewell to Archer, he steps out. A moment later, I hear the front door open and close as my brother leaves.

I do my best to ignore Archer, but I feel his gaze on me as I move around the living room, gathering the wineglasses and barely touched food.

"What are you doing here?" I ask finally as I head from the living room toward the kitchen.

"Hungry," he says, terse, even for him.

I shove the charcuterie board at him as I pass. "Here. Go crazy."

He follows me into the kitchen, already picking at some of the meats and cheeses on the board as he does so.

The wine my brother brought is excellent, so I pour myself a bit more. I very pointedly do not offer any to my neighbor, even as I regret a little that the easiness between us is gone. Even as I admit, only to myself, that I've missed him.

He sets the board on the counter, steadily making his way through its contents as he watches me, seeming to see way too much. I stand perfectly still at the opposite end of the kitchen island until he polishes off the last of the almonds.

"So. What are you supposed to be thinking about?" he asks finally.

"Hmm?" I say, taking a sip of wine.

"Your brother. He wanted you to think something over."

"Yup."

Archer looks frustrated by my atypical snippiness, but that's just too damn bad. He's made the rules. I'm just following them.

I fully expect him to give up and retreat back to his place, but he surprises me by trying again. "Job offer?"

I point at the empty board. "That enough to fill you up? I can make you a sandwich to go if not."

"I'm good." His eyes narrow slightly at the pointed inclusion of *to go.*

"Great." I pick up my wine and start toward the kitchen table, where some of my astrology books are laid out. I've been digging into the origins of Western astrology, and have been particularly engrossed with the Enlightenment era, when its legitimacy took its hardest hit.

Archer snags my elbow as I pass, drawing me around to face him. Startled by the contact, I look up into his eyes, finding a frustrated entreaty I've never seen from him before.

"Hey. Randy," he says, his voice brusque. "I know New Year's Eve was a mistake. *My* mistake. But . . . we can still be . . . friends. At least as long as you're living here?"

I only stare at him and slowly he releases his grip on my arm, though the warmth from his fingertips seems to linger even through the thick sleeve of my sweater.

"Right?" he says after a moment, and the brief flash of pleading in his eyes does something dangerous to my heart.

And I realize for the first time that Archer truly *is* a friend. Not just a neighbor I'm friendly with, but a friend. Someone I care about. Someone I don't care to hurt just because *I'm* hurt.

"Yeah. Yeah, of course," I say, softening my tone. "Of course we're friends."

His eyes search mine for a second, and though he nods, he doesn't look convinced. "Okay. Good. I'll let you get back to . . ." He waves toward my books.

"Archer," I say quickly before he can exit.

He turns back, and I hesitate only a second before sighing. I go to the fridge and pull out one of his favorite beers, which I somehow have found myself stocking over the past couple of months.

"My brother knows someone at Stanford," I say. "They want to interview me about a potential job."

He accepts the beer and takes a long drink before replying, seeming to think it over. "How do you feel about that?"

"I . . . have no idea," I admit, realizing that it hasn't even begun to really sink in. "Shocked, I guess. I never imagined that after getting denied tenure at Nova that another school of that caliber would even look at me again."

Archer remains silent, as though sensing I need to sort out my thoughts and giving me the room to do so.

"And I'm excited," I say after a moment, because it feels like what I'm supposed to be feeling. "I mean, it's tenure track. At Stanford."

"So you've decided that you miss it after all?" he asks. "The whole collegiate, academic scene."

"No," I say so quickly I surprise myself. Then I hold up a finger. "Let me rephrase. I still don't miss the politics of academia, or, if I'm being honest, the general dryness of the scholarly landscape. But I miss the other stuff."

"Other stuff," he repeats. "Teaching?"

"Yeah, I miss sharing knowledge with eager minds, but I also miss . . ."

I tug at my earring, too embarrassed to continue.

Archer leans over, elbows braced on the counter as he gives me a small smile. "Friends, remember?"

"Right. Okay." I take a breath and hold it for a second. "I miss the *other* stuff. The, um . . . The famous stuff. I miss being on TV. I miss guest hosting game shows. And the podcasts and the interviews and the documentaries. And it's not even about the fame, it's about *sharing* science. The scholarly community is tight knit, but sometimes it feels like there's an 'us and them' division between academics and nonacademics, which seems to sort of defeat the whole point. That knowledge is meant to be *shared*."

"Could you do all that stuff without also being a professor?"

I shake my head. "They go hand in hand. All the TV spots dried up the second word got out that I was denied tenure. I guess I'm persona non grata unless I have Nova behind me."

I haven't realized until now how much that's bothered me. I've been making excuses for months as to why *Good Morning America* stopped calling. And all the other shows and interviews as well. I've been telling myself there haven't been any meteor showers to discuss, no cool eclipses, and then there was the holidays . . .

But it's time to face facts. Nobody's calling me because I am nobody now.

"You think if you go to Stanford those offers will start coming in again?"

I shrug. "I'd like to think so."

"Stanford's in California." His eyes lock on mine as he points out this obvious but crucial point, and I nod, feeling a little hollow inside at the thought, and yet . . .

"I have to at least take the interview, right?" I say. "This is the path to what I've always wanted."

Archer straightens and scratches his jaw. "I'm surprised you're not consulting your horoscope. Doesn't that rule your life these days?"

I open my mouth, but he holds up a hand. "Hey. Don't get pissed. I'm just pointing out that you took a year to do this astrology thing. Shouldn't that be playing a role in your next career decision? If it does in other areas of your life?"

"Wait, I thought you hated astrology," I say, narrowing my eyes, remembering his furious reaction at my horoscope playing a part in our kiss. As though my *horoscope* was to blame for *the mistake*.

He hedges. "I don't hate it; I just think it's bullshit."

I roll my eyes. "Such a useful distinction."

Then I frown. "It feels weird to use astrology to make a decision that has to do with science."

He finishes his beer and drops it into the recycling bin with a shrug. "Your life, Randy. But from the outside? Seems like this whole year has been an exercise in learning how to trust yourself. Your *real* self."

For some reason, that simple sentence feels even harder to wrap my head around than a potential job offer from Stanford.

And a hell of a lot more unsettling.

"Wait, what? You just drop a deep nugget like that and leave?" I ask, unable to keep the disappointment out of my voice as he heads toward the front door.

He turns around with a slight smile. "For now. Working on a few pieces that are demanding just about everything I have."

"Oh, that's great! You're finally *consumed*," I say, echoing his own word over the way he wants to feel about his work.

"Yeah. Yeah, apparently, I am," he says a little quietly. He starts back down the hall again, then turns back once more. "Hey. Randy."

"Hmm?"

"What's Stanford going to mean for you and Christian? You going to try the long-distance thing?"

I'd just opened the fridge to make myself a salad, but I close it abruptly. Apparently I'm not *entirely* ready to move past New Year's Eve, because the question grates on the emotions that still feel raw from that night.

"Asking as a *friend*?" I ask, a slight edge creeping into my voice.

His blink lasts a split second too long, as though he didn't anticipate the question, or my tone. "Sure. Of course. What else?"

What else? The question says plenty and scrapes a little at my heart.

"I don't know what my future holds," I say simply.

It's a half-truth, because it doesn't feel fair to tell him I'm breaking up with Christian before Christian himself hears it.

And it's a half-truth because I do know one thing about my future:

Simon Archer doesn't seem to want a starring role in it.

AQUARIUS SEASON

The Sun moves into Aquarius today, darling Gemini, and with Aquarius being ruled by Uranus, stationed retrograde, rebellion and sudden change are on the horizon. If there's a hard conversation you've been putting off, now is the time for it. Clear the way for a season of reinvention.

The butterflies leading up to my first date with Christian have nothing on the butterflies leading up to what is to be my *last* date with Christian. But now, as with then, they dissipate the instant I'm in his company.

This time, their disappearance is bittersweet. A realization that lack of butterflies isn't always a good thing. Sometimes it can signal the absence of that certain *something*.

After what feels like the longest monologue of my life, he exhales and cups the mug between his two hands, giving me a rueful smile across my kitchen table. "I hope you'll take this as the compliment it is, but you're quite skilled at breaking up with people."

I let out a surprised laugh. "Am I?"

I decide against telling him that I'm apparently a natural, because I have exactly zero practice in ending a relationship. I'm not sure he'd exactly be flattered to learn that this is my first time.

Christian nods. "Normally there are either tears or yelling or half-truths about it not being personal. But I feel a bit like I've just been presented a set of empirical facts, to which there is no other explanation besides we aren't meant to be."

"If it helps, I really did *want* us to be," I say, meaning it.

He grins over his coffee. "Oh yeah? And you're *sure* I can't play the whole astrological compatibility card? That you and I are destined in the stars, and all that?"

I smile back, though it feels sad because *I'm* sad, if nothing else over the dream of what could have been. "That's actually a big part of why I need to put a stop to this, in addition to the Stanford thing. It was one thing to go on a date with you as an astrological experiment. But to let it keep going simply as part of an astrological study isn't ethical."

"But you've been open with me about that from the start," he says, leaning forward with a gentle half-joking, half-sad smile. He spreads his hands to the side slightly and playfully raises his eyebrows. "I'm a willing participant here, Miranda."

"Yes, but you're a willing adult," I say gently. "It's not just about you and me."

He blows out a sigh. "Kylee."

I nod. "We both know she's no longer looking at me as *just* her tutor."

His eyes shadow. He rubs a hand over his neck. "She did ask the other day if I was going to invite her mom to our wedding, or if I thought that would be weird."

I let out a startled, dismayed laugh. "Oh dear. So you see

my point. I can't let her keep hoping for a future that I just don't see happening. Especially if things work out with Stanford. I can't break her heart."

"It's inconvenient," Christian says, smiling, "that your reasons for breaking up with me make me like you even more."

"I like you, too," I say honestly. "But—"

"Yeah, yeah, I know," he says affably, holding up a hand and then standing. "Your skill at breakup speeches doesn't mean I want to hear it again. Ego, and all that."

Damn. He really is likable.

"Right. Of course."

I stand as well and walk Christian to the front door.

He opens the door, and, placing a hand on the doorjamb, drums his fingers thoughtfully as he looks at me.

"What's the other part?" he asks.

"Hmm?"

"You explained that you couldn't keep using me for the sake of your research. And let Kylee get hurt in the process. And the probable move to California. You said those were a big part of the reason you're breaking up with me. What's the other?"

"Oh." Maybe I'm not great at breakups after all, because my mind reels but I come up with a blank. "I don't know."

"Sure you do," he says with a small smile. "Or maybe you don't. But *I* do."

"You do?" I blink in confusion.

"Sure." Christian taps the door once with an open palm and steps out onto the porch before giving me a last one of those perfect, charming smiles. "He lives next door."

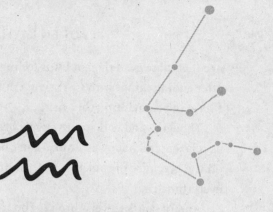

AQUARIUS SEASON

*The Waning Moon in Pisces is an ideal time to
indulge in some self-care. Treat yourself to the
facial or pedicure, but don't neglect to pamper your
emotional self as well. Changes lie ahead that will
require your head and heart to be in full alignment.*

Lillian insisted I come visit her in Florida. She claims it's
over concern for my vitamin D levels and a desperate need
for conversation that doesn't involve hemorrhoid cream or
yarn, but from the moment I've arrived, her real motive is
clear:

Assessing the damage following my breakup with Christian.

From the moment I arrived four days ago, it's been nothing
but Breakup Martinis (an unfortunate combination of rasp-
berry cordial, coconut rum, and gin), chocolate for dinner, and
movie marathons starring anything with Spencer Tracy and
Katharine Hepburn.

In any other situation, I'd have preferred wine, potato chips,
and Tom Hanks/Meg Ryan. But I'm solely in Lillian's orbit, and
her special brand of pampering is apparently exactly what I

need, because even though I was feeling far from brokenhearted after ending things with Christian, I'm feeling the most carefree I have in years during this visit.

Though—and perhaps it's simply because of my horoscope—as relaxed and happy as I am, I can't help but feel like I'm also on the precipice of something. A calm before a storm in which everything changes.

And of course, everything *is* about to change.

It may only be late January, but the end of my sabbatical is approaching—at least the unofficial date I've set for myself at the end of April. It's *not* quite the end of the official academic calendar, but it's close enough, and gives me a bit more time to shift gears toward my reentry into the academic world.

I'm not sure what it means that April feels awfully close. *Too* close.

I'm lying beside Lillian's pool, trying not to think about it, and obeying her command to "catch some rays," though I'm pretty sure the rays don't stand a chance of penetrating the thick layer of SPF I've slathered on.

Lillian steps out onto the patio and lets out a long whistle, reminiscent of a construction worker catcalling the heroine of an old movie. "I've been worried about your broken heart, but seeing you now in a bikini, I think it's the boy I should be worrying about."

I smile but roll my eyes good-naturedly behind my sunglasses. "Yes, I'm sure he's mourning my complete lack of curves."

"Voluptuous is only one version of sexy," she says, settling in an Adirondack chair beside me. "And you know, there is something *extra* going on with you since I saw you last. Not in your physical body, but your aura. What is it?" she asks.

"Could be the fact that I can actually sleep through the night on Friday nights now that I'm not living on a college campus?" I say, rising to my elbows and looking over at her. "Or perhaps the fact that I've been eating something other than turkey sandwiches from the school cafeteria for the first time in a decade? Or—"

"Fluidity," she says, snapping her fingers. "That's what I'm seeing."

I pull down my sunglasses to give her a bemused look. "What?"

"Ever since you started your academic march toward tenure, you've been so rigid. Always heading in one single direction, never looking side to side. Now you're more . . . *Relaxed* isn't the right word; that's too temporary of a state. But there's a lovely calm about you now. I wonder where that's stemming from." Her fingers drum the chair's arm as she considers this, rings tapping.

"I told you, sleep. Good food. No deadlines."

"Maybe," she says, mostly to herself. "Maybe. How are the Buzzes?"

"They're good," I say, startled by the sudden change in subject. "Great, actually. I moved them down to the greenhouse for a couple weeks there, but I took them back up to the roof. They seem happier there."

Her smile is smug.

"I know, I know." I flick my sunglasses back onto my nose. "You told me they liked the roof. I should have listened."

Her smugness only seems to increase, and I have the distinct impression that I'm missing something, but that's pretty much par for the course with my aunt.

She leans forward and pats my foot fondly, then stands.

"We need some nice iced tea. Then I'm going to give Judith a call about the bridge meeting tonight. I'll tell her to add an extra chair for you."

"Oh, please don't," I beg. "I have no idea how to play bridge."

"That big brain of yours? You'll pick it up."

I shake my head, resigned, because since I've been here, Lillian has declared that my "big brain" would make it easy for me to dominate at golf, pickleball, bunco, and bingo.

Needless to say, my "genius" status does very little to help me in physical activity or games built primarily on luck.

"Not *Belinda*," I hear Lillian say loudly from inside her kitchen. "*Miranda*. Like the lawyer from *Sex and the City* with the orange hair. Orange! Hair! Miranda's coming to bridge . . . bridge! Where's your hearing aid?"

I smile to myself as I reach over to pick up my buzzing phone. I expect it to be Daphne checking in, but I sit upright when I see the caller ID.

Stanford University.

I've been expecting this call—hoping for it? Dreading it? But now that it's here, I feel more confounded than ever.

Heart pounding, I take a deep breath, then answer. "Dr. Miranda Reed."

This used to be a title I used several times a day with pride. It's been months since I've been anything other than Miranda, and I feel a little pang of regret that soon I'll have to wear the full doctorate mantle again.

"Miranda, I'm so glad I caught you. This is Dr. Samuel Belmont. I'm the head of the Physics Department here at Stanford."

Here we go.

"What an honor to hear from you," I say in a crisp, modulated tone. It's harder than I expected to slip back into professor mode, and even though that was my persona for years, it feels a little foreign. Uncomfortable.

Probably just rusty, I reassure myself.

"I hope it's not too gushing to say how much I enjoyed your paper on topological quantum computing last year," I continue.

"Gush away; that one nearly killed me to get right," he says with a laugh that's not quite fake, but practiced. As though he's used that exact line a thousand times in the past.

"So, Dr. Reed," he says, his voice turning a bit more serious, but still kind. "I'd love to have a conversation about you joining us here at Stanford."

"I—wow." I struggle for the correct response. Knowing from Jamie that this opening was coming and actually *hearing* it are two very different things.

"I'm honored," I say truthfully. "But before the conversation goes any further, I need to make sure you understand—"

"I heard about the tenure board's decision at your current school. But I can also say it doesn't make the least bit of sense to me," he says. "I've read your work. I've *seen* your work. Your student assessments tell me you're the most universally adored professor I've seen in STEM in a long time. You're exactly the sort of associate professor I want in my department, and though I obviously can't guarantee the future, I think you'll find the tenure board here has different . . . values from your current university."

It's not a promise of tenure. I know that. But it's as close to one as I'm ever going to get, and to hear it coming from someone as respected as Dr. Belmont, from a school as revered as Stanford . . .

It should be a dream come true.

It *is* a dream come true, especially given the unexpected

rejection from Nova. It's the sort of second chance that feels too good to be true.

So why am I not *giddy*?

"We have an unexpected opening within the theoretical astrophysics and cosmology arena, specifically on the graduate side," Dr. Samuel says. "I know you're on a much-earned sabbatical now, but since we're looking for someone to teach a summer session as well, I'd love to put our conversation on the fast track. Would you have time for a couple of phone interviews over the next month? And assuming it feels like a good fit all around, an in-person meeting in April to discuss details?"

"Absolutely," I hear myself say without really meaning to say it.

I have the strangest sense that it's a different Miranda who's replied from the Miranda who just a few moments ago was talking with Lillian about the Buzzes. A Miranda who doesn't have time for a houseplant, much less a pet. Or a relationship. A Miranda who doesn't drink whiskey on the roof with a sardonic artist until the wee hours of the morning, or have cake for breakfast at her horoscope's behest . . .

"I'm thrilled to hear it," Dr. Belmont says. "I've got to get to a meeting, but I'll put my assistant in touch to start coordinating times."

"That's wonderful. Thank you so much. I can't tell you how grateful I am to even be having this conversation," Professor Miranda says.

"We're excited here, too. It'll be a new experience for us to have a celebrity in our midst."

A silent whisper remarks that if Nova University didn't want me because of my celebrity status, Stanford only wants me because of it. That nobody wants me for me.

I mentally shut it down and say goodbye to Dr. Belmont just as Lillian steps back out onto the patio with a tray. Apparently by iced tea she meant martinis, but at least from the look of them they're the regular kind of martinis, and not some disgusting coconut-gin concoction.

"Everything good?" Lillian asks, setting the tray down. She presses a finger between my eyebrows. "You've got a line. Frownie."

"No, no frown. That was Stanford."

Her graying eyebrows wing upward. "Stanford! Fancy. What do they want?"

"To hire me. Tenure track," I say, feeling a little guilty that I haven't mentioned it to my aunt before now, though the slightly pinched look on her face reminds me why I didn't.

My aunt says nothing for a moment as she stirs the martinis. "You must be thrilled. You said yes?"

"Of course. Well, to the interview process. It sounds like it's more of a formality than anything, but . . . wow." I set a hand to my fluttering stomach. "I can't believe this is actually happening."

"And what about your sabbatical? Following your horoscope?"

"I'll see it through," I say, meaning it. "I have until April. Who knows, maybe my horoscope will provide me the exact guidance I need to navigate all of this."

"You don't mean that."

"I do!"

She shakes her head and drops two olives into each glass. "You don't. Ten minutes ago, you might have. Ten minutes ago, you actually let yourself believe in the power of the universe and destiny and human instincts."

215

"And now?" I say defensively.

"And now"—she hands me a glass—"you're ready to return to your old ways. Where this reigns supreme." She taps my head. "And this is told to shut up." She presses her finger to my heart.

"That isn't . . ." I swallow, frustrated, and a little hurt by the lack of support. Lillian is my biggest cheerleader, and right now she seems almost disappointed in me. "Why are you so against this?"

My voice sounds desperate, and I realize it's not that I'm worried that my *aunt* is against it. It's that she's *right*. I'm trying to block out my heart's instincts because they're saying something my brain doesn't want to hear.

"Oh, honey." She sighs and sits down in the chair. "I'm not against anything that you want."

"Then be happy for me," I plead. "This is what I've always wanted. An academic setting to thrive in and grow . . ." My voice trails off, because I can't quite seem to think of all the reasons this is so important.

"Taking the same job you had before, on the same path, with the same goal, but in California—that's thriving? And growing?"

"Don't say it like that." My voice is a touch sharper than I mean it to be. "This is my dream."

She fishes an olive out of the glass, pops it into her mouth, and chews. "So you keep saying."

"Because it's true," I say, trying to ignore the fact that even to my own ears it sounds desperate, as though I'm clinging to the idea. "My career is all I have. It's who I *am*."

Lillian looks directly into my eyes. "Listen to me closely, because I'm older, and believe it or not, much smarter about some things. You're not a scientist, a person with two doctorates, or even a Gemini rising. You're not your parents' daughter or brothers' sister, Daphne's best friend, or even my favorite niece. Those are crucial parts of you, but they aren't who you *are*."

"So who am I?" I whisper in a soft voice I don't recognize.

She squeezes my hand. "The end of your Horoscope Project is coming soon. You'll find her. You'll find *you*."

♒ AQUARIUS SEASON

*Saturn trines Uranus, but you'll have a hard
time seeing things clearly today, darling Gemini.
Which is problematic because you're also feeling
spontaneous. Try for a compromise: give in to the
spontaneity but keep future you in mind before you
make any big leaps. Think temporary tattoo over
permanent, painting a room vs. buying a new house.*

Oh god, Randy. What am I looking at here?"

I glance over my shoulder at Archer. I've been so engrossed in my latest project that I didn't hear him come in.

"Archer." I gesture to the fish tank in front of me. "I'd like to introduce you to Andromeda."

Archer sighs and then comes up beside me, bending to brace both hands on his knees as he stares into the brand-new fish tank, which has a lone fish swimming inside it. "Andromeda. She's that orange guy hovering by the little castle?"

"Um, you mean Atlantis," I say. "Obviously."

"Obviously." He straightens and gives me a knowing look. "Horoscope?"

I nod. "It says that today was the perfect day for a pet. I mean, it didn't say that. But I'm getting very good at interpreting this the longer I do it."

"Uh-huh." He gives the fish a skeptical look.

"Okay, I know what you're thinking," I explain. "As far as pets go, a fish is a little boring. And I initially went to the amphibious category: snake, iguana. The usual suspects."

Archer slowly lifts a hand to cover his mouth. Nods. "Absolutely. The typical pets."

"But those require quite a lot of care," I explain.

"Right, of course. And dog or cat . . . they didn't enter the equation?"

"They did," I say a little wistfully. "I've always thought a cat and I would get along well."

"Okay. So, you've always wanted a cat, and yet . . ." He gestures at the simple fish tank I'd bought earlier this morning. "Goldfish?"

"Well, see, that's where the horoscope came in. It said I should give in to a spontaneous urge . . . that was the idea of getting a pet. But to *temper* the spontaneity by making sure it took future me into consideration."

Archer continues to look skeptical. "Future you wants a fish?"

"Well, I don't know." I sigh. "Not specifically, I guess. But future me will have a very different schedule. Once I go back to real life, I'll work crazy long hours. It wouldn't be fair to a cat to be gone all the time."

Archer tilts his head back slightly. "Real life."

"Yeah," I say, giving Andromeda a few flakes of food. "You know. Lecturing, writing, grading papers, the occasional interview."

"Ah." He crosses his arms. "So Stanford is officially a go."

"No," I say. "Not officially. But they called."

He nods. "And this is a good thing?"

"Of course it's a good thing," I say automatically. "It's Stanford. And tenure."

My voice sounds wooden.

"And what about the part where you said you didn't miss the academia stuff so much?" he asks.

"I think I was just a little nervous and out of practice. Practically speaking, we all have parts of the job that we tolerate so we can do the parts we do like. Right?"

"Randy, that sounds like someone trying to justify the fact that they're going through the motions for the sake of other people's expectations."

"Oh really," I say, crossing my own arms and facing him. "This from the guy whose current art series is acrylics of Paris? Even though he doesn't want to do travel pieces right now, and prefers charcoal?"

"I told you, nobody buys charcoal," he snaps.

"Exactly. And nobody hires a physicist whose academic career has stagnated to be a part of a National Geographic documentary."

Archer tilts his head. "We fighting, Randy?"

I laugh a little. "Apparently. I think Lillian's feistiness rubbed off on me while I was in Florida."

He looks like he wants to say more, but instead he rolls his shoulders as though making a conscious effort to drop the Stanford topic, even though he doesn't want to.

"How is she? Lillian," he asks. "How was the trip?"

"She's great. I had a good time."

I don't tell him that the final day after Stanford had called,

221

things had been a little less easy between my aunt and myself. I'd been frustrated by her inability to see that I'm making the smart decision. She'd seemed disappointed that . . . well, I don't know, precisely. I just know that every time she looked at me, there was a little bit of sadness.

I glance back at the fish tank. "Do you think I should have gotten Andromeda a friend?"

"You mean like someone to braid her tail fin? Be her designated driver when she's had too much to drink at Atlantis?"

"No. I mean so she doesn't get lonely. When I go back to real life."

"Real life," he repeats, the easy teasing of his tone vanishing. "That's the second time you've said that in the last five minutes. So all of this"—he gestures around Lillian's home—"these past few months, this hasn't been real life?"

"Well." I swallow, because suddenly I'm getting the same vibrations from him that I did from Lillian. Disappointment.

Except with him, it also seems tinged with disgust.

"I just mean . . . of course it's been real," I clarify. "But also, you know. Temporary."

He says nothing, and I keep talking.

"These past few months are a blip. A hiccup. A sabbatical, if you will."

"I see."

There's something completely new and unfamiliar in his voice now, and a tightness in his features that I haven't seen since New Year's Eve.

"I'm not saying this correctly," I say desperately. "I've made it sound like this time at Lillian's was some sort of cosmic mistake. What I meant was this has been a really, really nice vacation."

He says nothing.

"And a big part of what's made it so nice has been my new friend."

Still nothing.

"*You*, idiot," I say, exasperated. "*You're* the friend."

"Yeah, I got that."

"Then why?" I huff, frustrated. "Why do you look like that?"

"Like what? This is my face."

"No. I mean, yes, your face always looks like it's carved out of freaking granite, but you've put up, like, a wall."

"What, so you read people now? Not just star charts and nerdy papers?"

"See?" I gesture with a finger up and down. "I'm not even going to get mad at that, because I can see you're lashing out from behind your wall."

"I'm not . . ." He inhales deeply. "You're so annoying. I'm not lashing out. And there's no wall."

"Prove it."

He rolls his eyes upward. "I'm leaving. Andromeda, very nice to meet you. Miranda, let me know when you quit being weird."

"Prove it," I say again. "Prove that you're not trying to push me away. That we're still *friends*."

I put a slight emphasis on the last word. To remind him that he was the one who set those expectations.

Archer lets out a resigned sigh. "What do you want me to do? Write you a best-friend sonnet? Make you some sort of bracelet? Offer to feed your fish while you're away like I do your plants?"

"You'll do that last one anyway," I say with confidence, trying not to let myself think that that arrangement will only last as long as I'm here at Lillian's. Just a couple of more months, which suddenly seems like not nearly enough time for . . . for anything.

"I was thinking a hug," I say, even though I wasn't thinking it until just now. It just popped into my head, and I'm surprised by how much I want him to say yes.

"Not really a hugger," he says, giving me a wary look like he'll bolt at any time.

"Me neither, historically. Maybe we just need practice." Acting entirely on instinct and a need I can't define, I step forward and slip my arms around his waist. Archer stiffens immediately, but a half second later surprises me by relaxing. His arms close around my back.

I'm not sure if he pulls me closer, or I wiggle in of my own accord, but somehow what should have been a brief and simple hug feels more like an embrace that I never want to end. His stomach is firm and warm against my chest, and the way he glides a hand up over my spine, pressing his palm firmly between my shoulder blades, feels almost protective. *Possessive*.

I don't know how long the hug lasts. Or who gently shifts away first. But I know that when it's over, we don't quite meet each other's eyes. That that wasn't a normal hug between friends.

Most poignantly of all, the ache deep in my chest knows that this may not be real life.

But it's real *something*.

Something I'm terrified to name.

AQUARIUS SEASON

Today will not unfold as planned, dear Gemini.
Trust that what seems like a mishap is actually the
universe correcting itself, putting you back on the
path that you were meant to take. Your instincts
are spot-on, and every step you take now is a
necessary part of your journey toward
what you've been seeking.

Except for the couple of years I was with Daniel, Valentine's Day is my and Daphne's day. It started out as pizza and cheap rosé on the couch while she explained the nuances of reality TV to me. But the last two years, we've upgraded the whole affair.

We don't go out. The whole fixed-menu, reservations-required, stilted formality? Pass. But that doesn't mean that we don't go all out.

We dress up. We take turns cooking for each other, and we go *fancy*: scallops, caviar, filet mignon. Then there was the fancy ice cream and lobster rolls and *Thor* night last year.

As a result? I love Valentine's Day.

Truthfully, I've never really understood the whole bitter-because-I'm-single thing. I can be single. I can even *like* being single. And still enjoy romantic love and all the clichés that come with it—chocolate, roses, even sappy love songs. Daphne and I do it all together.

Until tonight.

"I'm so sorry, sweetie," Daphne says, though it's more of a croak-moan. "I seriously thought I was just tired this morning and the stomachache would pass, but just now as I was getting ready . . . I'll spare you the details."

"Don't apologize for being sick," I say firmly. "It's an affront to our friendship. You put on your baggiest, comfiest pajamas, lie down, watch something terrible, sleep. Whatever you need. Can I bring you anything? Crackers? Gatorade? Company?"

"I wish I could say yes, but I think I just want to go curl up in the bed and listen to my *Twilight* audiobooks."

I smile. Daphne loves *Twilight*. She's read the books and seen the movies more times than I can count, and it's her go-to whenever hungover or sick.

"Give Edward my best," I say.

"You're sure you're okay?" Daphne says, her voice slightly pleading. "I can't believe this is happening in a year when you just went through a breakup."

"I'm *really* good, Daph," I promise. I don't tell her that I've barely thought of Christian since, and even when I do, it's largely in relation to Kylee. For reasons I fully understand, Kylee's opted to pause our tutoring sessions, but it still stings a little. I miss her and the chance to talk to someone about the cosmos.

"Okay," she says reluctantly. "I love you. You know that."

"Always. Love you, too."

I hang up with my best friend and set my phone on the counter with the tiniest of sighs. I meant what I told Daphne. I would never be mad at her for having to cancel because she's sick. She could have canceled because she met a cute guy, and I *still* wouldn't be mad at her. That's just not how we operate.

But none of that changes the fact that I have an elaborate table for two set, and what I think is a pretty lovely baked Brie, beef Wellington, au gratin potatoes, and homemade chocolate soufflé waiting.

Not to mention my new red dress. One of my favorite stores had a sale and it felt made for me.

I glance in the direction of the fish tank. "I guess it's you and me, Andromeda."

I'd like to think she waves her tail at me in greeting as she glides by, but it's not much to work with.

Unless . . .

My eyes cut to my cell phone.

It's flirting with disaster. I know that. In a few short months, Simon Archer will be out of my life. Even if he weren't, he wants nothing to do with me romantically, and hanging out with him on Valentine's Day is only going to shine a big old spotlight on that.

Your instincts are spot-on, and every step you take now is a necessary part of your journey toward what you've been seeking.

"Alright, horoscope," I mutter. "You've gotten me this far."

I pick up my phone and call Archer.

It rings endlessly, and I'm about to end the call when he picks up. "Randy?"

"Hey."

A pause. "Everything okay?"

"Of course, why?"

"This is the first time you've ever called me. You either text or barge in.".

"*I* barge in?!" I shake my head, even though he can't see me. "Never mind. Is Alyssa in town today?"

Another pause. "No. Why would she be?"

I roll my eyes. "Oh, I don't know. Valentine's Day."

"Why would she be in New York City because it's Valentine's Day . . . Oh. Sure. Right. No, she's not here."

I roll my eyes upward. The man is the very opposite of a romantic.

"So, what's up?" he asks a touch impatiently. "Your dress zipper caught before a date with Christian?"

Even though it's been just a few weeks, my memories of Christian feel so faded and distant that the question catches me off guard.

"Christian and I broke up a few weeks ago."

There's another pause, even longer this time. "Oh."

I roll my eyes again. It's a good thing I wasn't expecting a bigger reaction, because I definitely didn't get it.

"Okay, so look," I say. "Daphne and I usually do a whole Galentine's thing together, but she came down with a nasty stomach bug. So now I have all this food, and . . . are you hungry?"

"On Valentine's Day?"

His wariness of the holiday is so purely *single man* that I rub a thumb between my eyebrows for patience. "Don't worry, I promise not to wait until the end of dinner before proposing."

"Does inviting me in Daphne's stead have anything to do with your horoscope?"

I blink. "Well, actually, now that you mention it—"

"Then no. Thanks for the offer, but I've got work to do."

He hangs up without waiting for my response, and even for Archer, it's abrupt. I pull the phone away and stare at it. "Alright then."

So, a solo night. I can make that work. Lots of practice.

I put my fancy baked Brie dish into the oven and try to decide between champagne and the nice red wine I've had decanting since noon. Mostly, I try not to dwell on the sharpness of Archer's rejection. I wasn't expecting him to fall all over himself to spend the hearts-and-flowers holiday with his platonic neighbor, but that the prospect was that distasteful . . .

I decide on champagne and am just pulling the foil off the cork when I hear a knock at the door. It's an unfamiliar noise. Daphne and Archer always just let themselves in. Christian always rang the doorbell. But a knock?

I go to the door and press my face to the peephole.

Immediately, I step back, my heart pounding. Archer?

I open the door and find a very irritable looking Archer on my front porch. He has a bouquet of purple flowers in one hand, a plastic bag in the other.

My eyes focus on the flowers first. "Are those from . . ."

"The Buzzes," he says, shoving the cut flowers at me. "Don't worry, I googled the proper way to cut them without damaging their growth."

"I . . . they're . . ." *So perfect.*

I shift my focus to the bag, which I now see holds a fish.

"Perseus," he says a little grumpily. "I actually got him this afternoon, before I realized it was Valentine's Day, so now it seems . . ."

"Romantic?" I say, batting my eyelashes.

He shoves the bag against my chest and steps into the foyer, immediately moving to the kitchen.

Then he stops. Steps backward so we're shoulder to shoulder. He jerks his chin at the fish. "That is not a love declaration."

My eyes go wide. "Oh, but it's practically Tiffany's!"

Only when he storms away with a grunt do I allow myself a smile.

Because it's better than Tiffany's.

Very carefully, I untie the top of the bag and let the pretty black goldfish join his new girlfriend in the fish tank.

"Perseus, huh? You know your Greek mythology," I call into the kitchen.

"Again, Google. Perseus saves Andromeda from a sea monster and . . . that's all I remember."

"They're also constellations," I say, joining him in the kitchen. "Perseus and Andromeda. Two of my favorites."

His eyes flick up. "I know. You've told me during one of your late-night rambles."

Have I?

I don't remember.

But he does.

Archer lifts the champagne bottle. "I saw that you've been tearing at the foil. Am I opening it?"

"Please," I say, turning my attention to my phone. I pull up the deliberately cheesy Valentine's Day playlist I'd put together that afternoon and connect it to the little Bluetooth speaker I keep on the kitchen counter.

A few seconds later, as the music swells, I hear the festive pop of a cork, and he pours us each a glass. I try not to remember that the last time I had champagne I was with him.

And that we kissed.

And that he very firmly told me it was a mistake.

"I thought you had to work," I say, accepting the glass with a smile of thanks.

"I did. I do. I am."

"What?"

"Nothing. Happy Valentine's Day, or whatever." He clinks his glass to mine and takes an irritated sip.

I take a sip myself, then pull the Brie out of the oven, feeling a little gratified at the way his eyes light up. I've added a layer of apricot preserves atop the puff pastry–wrapped wheel of creamy, decadent cheese, along with some chopped rosemary, thyme, and roasted pecans. I slide it onto a platter, which I've already prepped with fancy crackers and salted apple slices.

"So, Daphne's sick," he says, watching as I plate.

"Poor thing. Yeah."

"And Christian's . . . gone."

"Well not *dead*," I say. "Don't say it like that. It just didn't work out."

"Why not?"

I glance up briefly at the controlled intensity in his tone, then quickly back at the cheese. I lift a shoulder and try to keep my voice light. "Oh, you know. He has a daughter. Who wants a mom. I might be moving to California . . ."

"Might?"

I set the platter in front of him, as well as a side plate and silverware. He wastes no time digging in, making me realize that I'll miss this. Cooking for someone. I didn't even know I liked cooking for myself, but sharing a meal, whether it's fancy Valentine's Day fare or leftover chicken Parm, is an unexpected pleasure.

"I mean probably," I say quickly. "I won't know until the interview."

He nods, then gives me a once-over as he chews, as though seeing me for the first time. "You always dress like this for Daphne?"

I look down at my red dress with a smile. "Only on Valentine's Day. It's new. And expensive. But she's worth it." I look back at him. "Why'd you change your mind?"

"About?" He wipes his mouth with one of the red, glittery cocktail napkins I've set out.

"Tonight. You said you had to work. And hung up on me." I give him a patient look. "You know, right, that I wasn't trying to seduce you? You were my *backup* plan."

I break off then, distracted by the playlist I've put together of some of my favorite love songs. I let out a small, happy sigh at the opening notes of Nicole Henry's version of "Moon River."

He watches me. "Having a moment there, Randy?"

"Yes," I admit openly. "I love this song."

He looks at me a second longer, debating something, then he nods, almost to himself, and comes around the kitchen counter.

Wordlessly, he holds out a hand to me.

Wordlessly, I take it.

And then I'm dancing.

Dancing to a quietly old-fashioned love song on Valentine's Day, in my kitchen, with a neighbor who is a friend, who is . . . everything.

For now.

My cheek finds its way to his chest. His to the top of my head. His heartbeat warm and steady, his presence solid and so dear to me that I find my eyes watering.

"Randy," he murmurs, shifting his head slightly so his mouth brushes atop my head.

"Yeah," I whisper.

There's a moment of silence. "I have to work the next few weeks. A lot. You may not see much of me."

"Oh," I say, trying to hide my disappointment. We only have a few more months before I need to move—either to California, if the job works out, or back to the city, if Stanford doesn't want me and I return to Nova.

But I remind myself not to be selfish. My work has always been the most important thing to me. I can't begrudge him for feeling the same about his own.

The hand at my waist pulls me slightly closer, the thumb of his other hand brushing over mine. I don't think he's aware of it, which makes it sweeter somehow.

"I just . . ." He swallows. "I just want you to know. I'm not avoiding you, not really. I just need to go sort of heads-down on the art for a while."

"I understand," I say.

Though I'm not sure that I *do* understand. His words make sense, and I respect his creative process. But I feel like I'm missing something; that something else is going on that he can't tell me. Or won't.

For the next minute, we just dance. Except it doesn't feel like dancing so much as clinging to each other. To a moment we can carry with us when our lives inevitably diverge.

Finally, as the last of the music fades out, I start to step away, but his grip tightens, as though reflexively, holding me near.

"Archer?" I say softly, because I can feel conflict radiating from him; I just don't know the cause.

His jaw works for a moment, and then with an impatient shake of his head, he releases me and steps back.

"I've gotta get back," he says.

"Oh—sure," I say, disappointment mingling with confusion at his strange mood, even as I try to remember that he's probably just distracted by his work deadline.

Archer heads toward the front door, everything about him radiating an unnamed frustration.

He pauses before stepping out of the kitchen, bracing his palm on the doorjamb, giving it an impatient tap, before turning back around.

With purpose he walks back toward me, and for a thrilling moment I think he's going to kiss me, to claim my mouth with that same searing passion I felt on New Year's Eve.

Instead, when he dips his head, it's to brush his lips over my cheek. His mouth pauses near my ear, uttering a gruff whisper. "Happy Valentine's Day, Randy."

He steps back, and his walk out of the kitchen is more purposeful this time. He doesn't turn back.

"Happy Valentine's Day, Archer," I finally manage to echo, though the front door's already slammed shut.

I lift a hand to my cheek, a little startled to realize that I'm crying.

Because that *Happy Valentine's Day, Randy*?

It had felt an awful lot like goodbye.

ARIES SEASON

*The storm you've been subconsciously bracing for
bears down tonight, darling Gemini.
Not all is what it seems.*

Archer is good on his word. I *hate* that he is, but he is. I hardly see him over the next few weeks. Not coming or going from his apartment. Not from the roof.

Objectively, I know he's just hard at work, as he warned me he would be.

But it feels as though he's done with *me* in the process.

And perhaps that's for the best.

Because I need to be done with Archer, too.

I spend March in what feels like nonstop phone and video interviews with the entire Stanford Physics Department. Trying to impress without seeming like I'm trying to impress. Already identifying who's a Friday night happy hour possibility, and whom I should avoid at all costs.

The interview process is going well. I can feel it.

What I can't seem to feel is any particular excitement about it.

Achievement, yes. Pride, yes. It feels *good* to be wanted in the academic space again. To feel like the past twenty years of my life haven't been a waste of time.

But excited?

I'm working on that part.

Spring weather's been knocking at the door every so often for the past couple of weeks, so I've been spending more and more time up on the roof lately. With my telescope.

Alone.

Well, I have the Buzzes.

But somehow the stars through my telescope seem a little less bright without the man and his charcoal on the neighboring roof.

Which is why, on a clear, mild evening in early April, when I come up to water the Buzzes, I draw up short at the sight of him, the man I haven't seen in over a month. Archer's hands are in his pockets, his head tilted backward as he looks up at the clear night sky.

He doesn't glance my way. Of course he doesn't. He's Archer.

And yet, no part of this annoys me.

It's simply him.

As he is.

He's just . . . Archer.

I try to play it cool. As if the last time I saw him it wasn't Valentine's Day, and we hadn't danced, and it hadn't felt like . . . *something*.

"No easel tonight," I say very casually, since there are no art supplies in sight.

He holds up his right hand without looking over. "Trying to prevent hand cramping. I'm putting the finishing touches on my series today and forgot to take breaks."

"Oh, that's great," I say with enthusiasm, despite my mood. "Not the hand cramp. But finishing the series."

Archer nods in acknowledgment, then hesitates a moment, as though debating something.

Finally he walks toward me, stepping up to the ledge of his roof so we're face-to-face. He reaches into the back pocket of his jeans and pulls something out. Wordlessly, he hands it to me.

I take the black envelope from him and look down at the fancy wax seal with what I now recognize as the elaborate *A.* that serves as his signature. "Fancy."

He gives an indifferent shrug, though the tension I feel radiating off him belies the casual gesture.

I slide a thumb under the envelope's flap to open it and pull out an elegant invitation.

"It's for my art show in SoHo in a couple weeks." He shoves his hands into his back pockets. "They'll be revealing my new series."

"Oh, wow. *Wow.* I'm so happy for you! I can't—"

I break off when I see the date of the show, feeling my heart sink in my chest. "I fly out to California that evening. My interview's the next afternoon."

His head tips backward slightly as he inhales. "So, you're doing that."

I sense a tinge of disappointment, as though he expected better of me, and I feel myself shift into a defensive stance, physically and emotionally.

"If by *that* you mean pursuing my dreams, then yeah," I say, a sharp edge slipping into my voice.

In response, he merely gazes at me, and my temper flares.

"Okay, let's recap tonight's interaction," I say, wagging a finger between us. "You tell me about a major career accomplishment, and I'm over the moon for you. I do the same, and you can't even pretend to be excited for me?"

"Bullshit," he says quietly.

My mouth opens in protest, but he steps closer, his eyes flashing with anger.

"You're not looking for congratulations, and you don't need me to be excited for you," he continues. "You want someone to reassure you that you're doing the right thing, to tell you what to do and how to live so you don't have to make any actual decisions about your own life."

"I—"

"Because that's what you *do*, Miranda," he says, more animated and angrier than I've ever seen him. "You make your life through a paint-by-numbers system. Someone else draws the lines, and you just follow instructions."

"That's absurd."

"Yeah?" He crosses his arms and bends slightly so his eyes are level with mine, daring me to dig deeper. "So, you remember making a conscious decision to become a physicist? To go into academia? To pursue tenure track? Or was that merely a prescription that you followed to a T?"

"*Maybe*," I say. "Maybe you're right about that. Maybe I did pursue tenure a bit blindly in the past. But at least I can admit it, and course-correct. And let's not forget that I took an entire year to deliberately step away from that so-called paint-by-numbers life."

"*Wrong*," he says furiously. "You think your Horoscope Project was brave and bold, and maybe it *could* have been.

But all you did was swap one rule book for another. This wasn't about you putting your faith in the universe having a plan for you. This was about you needing another step-by-step instruction manual after your last one didn't go the way you hoped.

"Every part of your time here has been scripted," he continues. "From your fish, to your meal choices, to who you want to be with. I've refused to be a part of that script, and guess what? I refuse to be part of the next one as well. You want to switch back to following the academic rule book because it's easy, go for it. But don't expect a standing ovation from me."

Every word lands a painful blow upon my very soul, and there are whispers of truth in there that I'll agonize over later.

But not before I make a few points of my own.

"You want to talk about *easy*, Archer?" I ask. "Who's the one who's locked himself away from the world so he won't have to deal with it? You pretend it's just part of being an eccentric, isolated artist, but we both know what it really is."

His eyes narrow in warning, but I ignore it, because suddenly I see him. I see so clearly what's been right in front of me.

"You got *hurt*," I say. "Your fiancée *hurt* you. But instead of admitting that—even to yourself—instead of owning it and healing, you use it as an excuse to shut down, to pretend like nothing matters to you.

"You think your relationship with Alyssa is *casual*?" I continue. "It's not casual. It's not some modern, *adult* relationship, Archer. It's cowardice, plain and simple. It's so you don't have to go all in on another human being who might hurt you like

Willow hurt you. I may play by a rule book, but at least I'm in the game!"

My outburst ends on a shout, my heart hammering hard in my chest.

Archer doesn't move, aside from clenching and unclenching his jaw, as we stare at each other in anger and frustration for several long, emotionally charged moments.

"You done?" he asks finally, his voice low.

I swallow and nod because my throat aches with the threat of impending tears. "Yeah. Yeah, I'm done."

"Good. Because you and me. This. *We're* done."

I have a halfhearted impulse to point out there is no *we*. That there's nothing to end because nothing ever started.

But I know it isn't true.

Whatever's developed between Archer and me these past few months may not have a name, but it's the most real thing I've ever experienced with another person.

The most intense.

The most rewarding.

The most painful.

"Good luck with the interview, Randy," he says. "I hope you find everything you're looking for."

Archer walks away then, and I let him, because while I don't agree with his entire assessment, he's not wrong about me being on a path that doesn't include him. I know what my next few years will entail. I'll have to work harder than ever to prove myself after a failed tenure bid. From another state. In another time zone.

I don't need my horoscope or our incompatible natal charts to know that Archer and I aren't meant to be. Were never meant to be.

But after his door has shut with a slam, after he's gone, I slowly lower to the cold iron chair on the roof and finally let the tears fall.

Because I can't shake the feeling that everything I'm looking for?

Just walked away for good.

ARIES SEASON

*You'll be feeling the Full Moon in Scorpio tonight.
It may be time to let go of a grudge or baggage
that hasn't been serving you. Make room for
new beginnings.*

You guys really didn't have to come see me off," I tell my family, still in a bit of shock at their unexpected arrival. I leave for California tomorrow for my Stanford interview and had planned on a quiet night of packing.

Not just for the trip. But *packing* packing. Because if all goes well, I have a cross-country move ahead of me. And even if it doesn't go well, I still plan to move back to the city to resume a lecture position at Nova. Win-win.

But just as I'd been debating between ordering pizza and making scrambled eggs for dinner, my family had shown up at Lillian's front door in a scene right out of a movie finale. They have since whisked me away for a good-luck dinner at an Italian restaurant on the Upper East Side.

"Don't get too excited. It was only an hour-long flight," my brother Brian says, not looking up from his menu.

I smile as my mother swats him on the back of his head, a gesture I haven't seen since we were kids.

"Seriously?!" Brian says, rubbing the back of his head. "What the f—"

He catches her glare, then gives me an apologizing smile. "We were happy to make the trip, however long, sis."

"Uh-huh," I say, though I smile back. "But seriously, you guys. I really appreciate the support."

"We know. You *cried*," Jamie says, smart enough to dodge when my mom's hand comes for his head.

"Okay, in my defense, the entire family has never come to New York. Ever. I mean, I'm grateful, but—"

"We were afraid you'd tell us not to come," Mom says. "Especially after Christmas."

I reach out and squeeze her hand with a reassuring smile. "I'm thrilled that you're all here. It really . . . it means a lot."

Jamie waggles his eyebrows. "You nervous?"

"So nervous," I confide, and I can tell from the quick glances between my parents that they're surprised by my admission. We Reeds don't do nervous, we don't do doubt, we don't do . . . vulnerability. At least not externally.

But while I may not have much time for reading my horoscope in the future, or assessing potential boyfriends' natal charts, I can't deny that this past year—shedding the scientist cape, entering the whimsical world of astrology—has changed me.

It's allowed me to accept that there are facets of my personality, of my person, of my very soul that can't be explained or rationalized.

Because there is no *logical* reason I should be nervous about the upcoming interview. Intellectually, I know it's just a formality. Dr. Samuel himself has indicated that we'll be discussing compensation, which tells me the job is mine for the taking. That come summer term, I'll be a Northern California resident.

But that doesn't erase the fact that emotionally, my stomach is tied up in knots. Exposing that part of myself to my family, while a little foreign, feels surprisingly . . . good.

"Did you know I went to school with Dr. Chang?" my father asks from beside me. "He'll be on the interview panel. You'll have to tell him I say hello. It might help."

"Sure, of course."

"I heard Dr. Lena Goodrich will be there as well. I'd like to pick her brain," Brian adds.

"You'd like to pick more than that," Jamie mutters under his breath, this time failing to dodge my mother's swipe.

My dad ignores his sons and gives me an encouraging smile. "I think your chances are looking good. And even if this doesn't work out, you'll still land on your feet. Find something even better."

"I appreciate that."

"Don't thank me. It's just the way the stars have written it," my dad says, looking adorably eager as he pulls his phone out of his blazer pocket. "Check this out. I did your whole chart reading, and there's just no way the next few months don't hold good things for you."

I lift a hand to my lips to hide my affectionate smile before looking around the table. "So, exactly how aggressive was my tantrum on Christmas?"

"You reminded me of lightning," says my sister-in-law Emily, sounding a bit awed. "I thought you were going to channel all the energy from the cosmos and set the table on fire."

"You were intense," Jamie agrees. "It was cool, actually. Seeing beneath the mask a bit."

I smile because I know it's true. I had been living behind a mask.

And the past few months, I feel like I've just started to shed it. To learn who Miranda really is, and yet . . .

My disastrous conversation with Archer continues to loop through my head.

Wondering if I haven't really grown at all. If I'm not just putting on a different mask and calling it improvement.

"You were quite right to chastise us," Mom says, surprising me. "We've had some uncomfortable conversations since December, and I think we've all come to realize that our family value system can be a bit . . . rigid. And we got you something. A little good luck token." My mother slides a small box across the table.

"Oh. Wow," I say, because my family is not big on spontaneous *anything*, and now I have a spontaneous visit *and* a surprise gift.

I tug the white ribbon and flip open the tiny jewelry box to find a pair of delicate gold earrings. "Scorpio," I say, recognizing the constellation's symbol immediately.

"I know that you're a Virgo sun," Mom says quickly. Nervously. "And the important one, the ascendant, is Gemini. But your aunt told us that your moon sign was a Scorpio. And that the moon sign is what rules your emotions. Your intuition. It's what we've all seen you get in touch with this past year. And it's what we're all most proud of. Whatever happens tomorrow . . . we're proud of you."

Through a haze of tears, I see the rest of my family nod in

agreement. And I'm touched by the gesture and the sentiment. More than I'll probably be able to express.

But as I stare down at the delicate jewelry, I also have to bite back the protest that I haven't earned these. Not really.

I may have faced some of the emotions. But not the big ones.

Not the ones that could change everything, if I were only a *little* bit braver.

TAURUS SEASON

*Prepare for a seismic shift, Gemini, as the world
will throw you a curveball challenging the very
foundations of your belief system. This upheaval is
uncomfortable but necessary; use its momentum
to build new, stronger truths.*

The next evening, my 5 p.m. flight to California is delayed by a couple of hours. Since the actual interview isn't until tomorrow afternoon, I shouldn't be worried. Even with the delay, the three-hour time difference means I'll land in San Francisco well before midnight. Plenty of time to get a good night's sleep and review my notes in the morning.

And I'm not *worried*. Not about the flight, or the interview. I'm just . . . jittery. I have been all day, and I can't quite figure out why. My brain has gone through every scenario, reassured me that everything is in order. But it feels a bit like logic is warring with instinct.

And instinct seems to be getting the edge, because the closer I get to my flight's departure, the more I sense that something's *off*.

Or maybe it's just my horoscope. A seismic shift?

Really?

Right as I'm heading to a city located smack on the San Andreas Fault?

But of course my horoscope's probably not talking about San Francisco's dicey earthquake history. It's talking about some other seismic shift, and I've had enough of those lately. I'm ready for stability.

I shift in the creaky, fake-leather chair outside my gate, but my legs feel restless, as though they're itching to run away from the airport.

Or toward something.

I cross my legs and stubbornly refuse to allow so much as an idle foot waggle.

When my phone buzzes, I all but lunge for it, desperate for distraction. I don't recognize the number, but I pick it up anyway.

"Hi, this is Miranda."

My own greeting catches me off guard.

Where's my usual, crisp *Dr. Miranda Reed*?

"Miranda! Hi! This is Alyssa Upton. We met on New Year's Eve?"

"Oh! Hi," I say, setting both feet on the ugly airport carpet and sitting up a bit straighter.

"I know this is out of nowhere, but is this an okay time? I'd love to run something by you."

"Um. Sure?" I say, though I can't imagine in what part of the multiverse Alyssa and I would have anything to discuss.

Unless it's about Archer.

In which case I will claim that my cell phone was stolen

right out my hand and disconnect, because I am *not* having that conversation. Not with his . . . whatever they are.

Still, I glance at the screen with my flight information. It's now *three* hours delayed. "Sure, I've got some time."

"Okay, *great*," she says with the kind of warm enthusiasm that feels genuine, like I've just made her whole day by giving her a couple of minutes of my time.

This woman is really hard to dislike, and trust me, I've given it some effort.

"So, listen, at the risk of sounding stalkerish, I've totally been creeping on every corner of the internet and YouTube for every appearance you've ever done, and let me just say, Miranda—you're fantastic."

"Um. Thank you?"

"No, I mean it. You're engaging, so smart but never condescending. You have a real knack for making even the most complicated concepts feel manageable. After watching you for hours, I felt like I was ready to give a TED Talk on black holes."

Black holes aren't exactly one of the brain busters of my area, but I can appreciate the point she's trying to make. "Thanks. That's really nice to hear. Especially since that particular part of my career seems to have dried up."

"Yeah, about that," she says. "So, I hope you don't mind, but some of the producers you've worked with are in my black book, so to speak, and I got in touch. Were you aware that your university has been telling them you're unavailable?"

Those. Assholes.

My lips part in genuine surprise. "I—no. No, I had no idea. I figured that they'd found someone to fill the science spot, because I haven't heard about a single request."

She makes an irritated noise. "Someone probably was hoping for their own moment in the spotlight. But they're wasting their time. Honey, you're a unicorn, and the people that make the decisions know it. Which is why I have to ask: Have you ever thought about doing that side of things full-time? The media thing?"

"No. Never," I say in all honesty. "Even at my busiest, the demand for someone to talk about meteor showers or explain the latest discovery at CERN only came in a couple of times a month."

"Right, oh my gosh, you'd be so bored if that's all it was. But what if there was more out there . . . like, a lot more?"

"A lot more . . . interviews?" I'm not following at all.

"So, okay, this is a bad business move on my end, since I'm not officially representing you yet, and you could take this to another agent and I'd be screwed, but I happen to know a new game show, a new docuseries, and even a talk show that would all kill to have you as their host. And don't even get me started on the opportunities that would open up if you had your own podcast. You could do the Bill Nye thing . . ."

"I . . . Wow."

"It's a lot, I know. And I'm so sorry to spring this on you, but Archer mentioned it to me like a month ago, but I just now got around to looking into the possibilities, and I got so excited—"

"Wait. Archer put you up to this?"

"Well, yeah. I mean, you know Archer. It was more command than request, and I only had about ten words to go on. But he seemed to think it might be something that you'd be open to at least exploring."

"I've never . . . I'm actually pretty far along in the interview process for another academic position," I tell her. "Could I do . . . both?"

I hear her take a sip of a drink, sensing that she's considering my question seriously. "Honestly, I don't think so. I mean, you can! You can keep doing what you're doing, showing up whenever there's a special harvest moon, or whatever. But the bigger gigs, the things that would make you fully a household name . . . those would require a lot more of your time than you'll have if you're a full-time professor."

"I don't care about being a household name."

She lets out a laugh. "Archer said you'd say exactly that. And that I should tell you that it's not about eyeballs. It's about minds. Lots of them. Ready to be blown away by star stuff. But hold on—let me check my notes, because he told me to say something else . . . He said it would help you stay sharp on the cosmos?"

I laugh a little, because it's the exact same awkward phrase I'd used in my failed attempt to flirt with Christian all that time ago. My laughter feels a little raw, however, because it's uncomfortable to realize just how well Simon Archer knows me. How well he listens. How much he sees, even when I don't see it myself.

Because listening to Alyssa talk about all these possibilities? Assuming she's not blowing smoke?

They light something inside of me that the prospect of tenure at Stanford doesn't.

That the prospect of tenure never did.

"I need some time to think all this over," I say. Because it's not like my whole personality has been a sham. I'm still rational at my core.

"Of course. Of course. Just . . . promise me I get first shot at putting my hat in the ring to be your agent."

"Absolutely," I agree, because I like Alyssa, even if I don't particularly love the fact that she and Archer sleep together whenever it suits them.

Realizing that I haven't expressed even a modicum of interest in whatever's going on with Alyssa, I try to remember my manners and reciprocate conversationally. "How have things been with you? You and Archer do anything fun for his birthday?"

There's a long pause. "His birthday. You mean back in December?"

"No." My regard for her slips just slightly for not knowing his birthday. However casual they are, that seems like it should be on her radar. "It was just last week. April 10."

An Aries.

Alyssa lets out a little laugh. "Sorry, babe, but I am one hundred percent sure it's December 2. I'm *positive*, because the year before last he had to go get his license renewed and was grumpy about it."

"Archer's grumpy about everything," I say distractedly, even as my brain tries to sort this out. "Why in the world would he lie to me about his birthday?"

"Not a clue," she says breezily. "He and I stayed friendly after we broke up—I mean, the guy let me use his house for New Year's Eve, for god's sake. But we don't chat as much as we used to."

"You . . ." I'm too stunned to say anything else. *Here's* the curveball my horoscope promised.

"You broke up?" I manage. "When?"

"Oh gosh. Forever ago," she says, distracted, and I hear someone else trying to get her attention.

"*When?*" I press, and the instincts that have been crackling all day are on full alert now, screaming at me that this detail is important. Crucial.

She seems to sense my urgency, because I feel her attention snap back to me fully.

"Okay, well, let me think," Alyssa says. "It must have been back in late August, maybe early September? I can't remember exactly. He just said he needed to end our arrangement because something had changed for him. He never would tell me what."

And there it is. My seismic shift.

That something that had changed for Archer?

It was me.

TAURUS SEASON

*A common thread in the astrology community
is the idea that the universe has our back.
All we have to do is listen to the signs.*

I've never quite bought it. Never quite let myself believe that there are mysterious energies at work, guiding us. Helping us.

But on my mad dash from JFK to Manhattan to try to catch the tail end of Archer's big night at the art gallery? I start to become a believer.

The wait for my Uber is one minute. The rainstorm that's been causing all the flight delays lets up the second I step out of the airport. Traffic back into the city is almost comically nonexistent. And we make every single light.

The universe does indeed seem to have my back.

Right until the final moment.

When it's just not enough.

Daphne is sitting on the steps of the SoHo gallery. She'd been tickled to learn from her connections in the art community that Archer had specifically requested that she receive an invitation. She'd accepted before things turned sour between Archer and myself, but I'm still glad that she went.

That at least someone was there for him. Supporting him.

I can see from her face and the dark building that I'm too late.

My eyes immediately flood with tears and I swipe at them, suddenly furious at the universe. At myself. "I wanted . . . I so wanted. Now he won't know . . ."

"Oh, sweetie, it'll still mean a lot that you tried," Daphne says, coming toward me, dressed in a stunning orange halter dress. She pulls me in for a long hug.

"Everyone left about a half hour ago. I tried to stall things, asking like a million questions, but the champagne was gone, there were no pieces left to sell, and most critically, the guest of honor left the first chance he got."

"But it went well?" I ask, pulling back from the hug and wiping my runny nose. "If there were no pieces left, that means they all sold, right?"

She takes my hand and squeezes it. "Okay, so listen, I actually know the guy who owns this gallery. And he owes me a favor from when I let him stay late at the Maya Patel exhibit at MoMA a couple years ago, so I called in a favor."

She holds up a set of keys.

"Are those . . ."

"For the gallery, yep. Because, sweetie, there's something you *really* need to see."

I follow her up the steps, and she unlocks the dead bolt and taps the alarm system keypad.

Daphne flicks on the light as I step into the trendy art gallery, but she stops in the doorway and doesn't follow me in. As though she's giving me space for whatever I need to see.

I blink, letting my eyes adjust.

I move fully into the main space, spinning in a slow circle as I take in each piece of Archer's new series.

I've started crying again, but don't realize it until I make a loud hiccupping noise that echoes throughout the room. "He didn't do Paris."

"No," Daphne says softly. "He sure as hell did not."

"And not acrylics, either."

"There's actually a *little* in there," she says, gesturing to one of the pieces. "The leaves here. He uses a bit of color to capture fall. And the moon in each piece. A touch there as well. But the majority of it is just charcoal. I didn't even realize he worked with charcoal, much less that he does some of the best work any of us have seen since Seurat."

I have no idea who Seurat is, and really don't care.

"I did. I knew," I say quietly. "Though he never let me see his work."

"Well, maybe now you can see why. *You* are his work. You're Archer's muse, Miranda."

I don't know anything about art. Or muses. But on this, I know she's right.

Archer's new series is twelve pieces. Each featuring the night sky. Each with its own zodiac sign. Each with a woman in motion. Watering plants in Aries. Feeding a goldfish in Pisces. Writing. Laughing.

A Capricorn kiss.

The woman. Me.

"All of this," I say, wiping my nose. "And I wasn't here. He invited me, and it was important, and I said no. I chose work."

"Admittedly, the guy is hard to read," Daphne says slowly. "But if I had to guess, I don't think he would have wanted you

259

to give up your work for his. I think he wants you to be happy. He didn't want to distract you from what you wanted."

I look at my best friend. "I want *him*."

"I know." She grins. "So get him."

I'm already shaking my head. "It's late. Really late."

Daphne gives me a gently chiding look. "Sweetie, not a single one of these drawings doesn't feature the night. Late night is sort of what you two do."

I feel a little flare of hope, because she's right.

And I know exactly where he'll be.

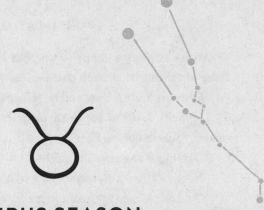

TAURUS SEASON

The thirty-minute drive from SoHo to Hudson Heights feels a million times longer than the six-hour flight to the Bay Area that I never got on. I try to use the time to figure out what to say. How to say it. Even as I make the familiar climb up the narrow steps to my rooftop, I don't have a clue.

But when I open the door and see Archer standing on my roof, words don't seem to matter as much as the fact that he's *there*.

With his beloved Michter's whiskey on the table.

And two mason jars. *Two.*

As though he's waiting for me.

As though he's always been waiting for me.

I quietly close the door behind me, and Archer glances my way, his eyes flashing something unreadable in the dim light.

"I thought we were done," I say quietly, repeating his parting words to me the last time we were up here.

Without a word, he pours some of the whiskey into a mason jar. He hands it to me.

"You knew that I'd come?"

"Hoped," is all he says. Gruffly.

My heart gives a happy flutter, but I tamp it down. I know there are things that need to be said. Most of them by me.

"I saw your art," I say softly. "Heard that it all sold."

He looks down at me in surprise, blue eyes reflecting confusion. "Who told you that?"

"Daphne. I thought she said—"

"None of it sold. Because none of it's for sale."

"Oh. *Ohh*. Weren't people upset they couldn't buy anything?" A distressing thought occurs. "Or did they not want to buy anything?"

The corner of his mouth twitches. "Oh, they wanted to buy them. But they're shit out of luck. Some things aren't for sale." He lifts a shoulder. "They'll get over it."

"What are you going to do with them?"

"I don't know yet." His gaze finds mine and holds it for a long moment before looking away.

I nod, then take another breath. "I got a call from Alyssa. Before I got on the plane. It was nice of you to point her in my direction. The opportunities she mentioned sound . . . incredible. Beyond my wildest dreams, actually."

Archer nods in acknowledgment.

"Why didn't you tell me?" I say after a moment. "That you and Alyssa haven't been together since—"

"Since I met you?" he asks, cutting his gaze over to me once more.

I swallow, nod.

"Because I knew you'd start asking questions. And that you weren't ready for the answers."

"I'm ready for them now," I whisper.

Archer takes a sip of whiskey, seeming conflicted, as though fighting some internal battle. His gaze searches my face before he seems to decide whatever he needs to decide and sets his drink on the table. He reaches into his pocket, fishing around until he comes up with a little scrap of paper.

"What's this?" I say, setting my drink aside as well and accepting the paper.

"My birthday."

I give him a knowing look. "You mean the one that's definitely *not* in April?"

He gives a quick crooked smile, not looking the least bit contrite. Then his expression turns serious as he nods down at the paper. "Open it."

I look down at the scrap, but don't unfold it. "Why would you lie about your birthday?"

Archer exhales. "You were right the other night. Willow did hurt me. It hurt that whatever she felt for me wasn't strong enough to combat whatever plans she thought the universe had for us. So I decided I wasn't ever going to put myself in that position again."

He rubs a hand over the back of his neck. "And then you came barging onto my roof, and . . . everything changed. But you were so damn hopeful that Christian's and your charts would align, and I realized . . . I was just the practice round. And I figured if I wasn't going to be a contender, I'd at least bow out on my own terms. That if we weren't a match based on a *fake* birthday it would sting less."

I make a sound of dismay. "Archer—"

"No, don't apologize," he says, holding up a hand. "You've been perfectly clear about your goal for this year. I may not get the whole star-chart thing, but I respected it was something you needed to do.

"And I told myself," he continues slowly, watching me, "that all I had to do was *wait*. Wait until you realized . . ." He runs a hand through his hair, looking frustrated. "Until you realized it didn't *matter* what our charts said. Until you chose me . . . for me."

I suck in a breath, my heart breaking at the raw vulnerability on his face, though there's something I'm still not understanding. I lift the paper. "Then why give me your real birthday now? Why not just wait until I was done with the horoscope thing?"

His eyes lock on to the paper. "Because I realized I wanted a chance before you made that decision on Stanford, even if it was only a sliver of one. A chance that our charts form a heart or whatever."

I smile. "Not really how it works." My thumb flicks over the paper, still not opening it. "And if we're *not* an astrological match?"

He steps closer, his eyes blazing as he lifts a hand to my face, thumb rubbing tenderly over my cheek. Expression pleading. "Would it matter? Miranda?"

It's a moment.

It's *the* moment.

In response, I lift the paper between us and slowly, deliberately tear it into tiny, unreadable little pieces.

He lets out breath that sounds almost like a gasp, and even as I hold scraps of his irrelevant birthday, Archer's hands slide into my hair, tilting my face back, as his mouth closes over mine in a hungry kiss. I release the last bits of paper, and with a groan of my own, grasp his shirt, pulling him closer and kissing him with months' worth of what I now, finally, can identify.

Love.

Archer presses a thumb along my jaw, adjusting the kiss so his tongue can slip between my lips, brushing against mine in a teasing, heated promise, and I let out a low moan.

He ends the kiss slowly, reluctantly, though his gaze doesn't leave my mouth quite yet, as he stares at my swollen lips greedily. For the first time, I'm not loath for our time on the roof to end. But I don't think I'll mind going back inside tonight. Not if Archer comes with me.

"You know," I murmur as my fingers explore his scratchy jaw. "I'm pretty sure Lillian moved the Buzzes up here on purpose. So we'd meet."

He snorts. "You think? The woman embodies the very idea of matchmaker."

"You knew?" I say in surprise. "That the flowers didn't need to be on the roof?"

Archer smiles. "From the very first night."

"Why didn't you say anything?" I ask, exasperated. "You could have just told me, and you could have had your quiet rooftop back!"

"I could have. But then I got a little busy."

"Doing what?"

Archer smiles and brushes his lips over mine. "Falling in love."

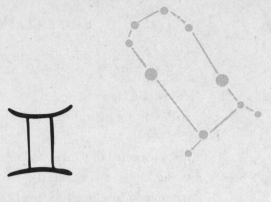

GEMINI SEASON

ONE YEAR LATER

A rcher?" I call as I step into our foyer and drop my keys
onto the entryway table. "You back yet?"

As I wait for his response, I slip off my high heels and shrug
out of my pale pink blazer. I've spent the entire day in Manhattan doing interviews as part of the publicity circuit for *The
Universe Unraveled*, my very own TV show in which I break
down complicated physics concepts for nonscientists. It's not
explicitly aimed at kids, but one of my stipulations before signing was that we ensure children would be able to follow along.

At my request, Kylee had been a part of the beta program
to make sure we were successful. She loves the show, though
maybe not quite as much as she's loving the fact that her dad
asked her to be his "best girl" at his upcoming wedding to a
lovely civil engineer named Lila.

The Universe Unraveled won't start airing until the fall,
but Alyssa tells me early reviews have been great, so much so
that the network's already picked it up for three more seasons.

The most popular episode in the prerelease for critics, and my favorite?

"Horoscope Hypotheses."

I still, waiting for any sign that Archer's in the home. *Our* home.

Lillian relocated to Florida and refused to sell me her house. Instead, she *gave* it to me.

Archer and I live here full time, and his house is now completely converted into his studio. He needs the extra space, after his *Miranda in Retrograde* series was a viral phenomenon in the art world. He still refuses to sell a single piece, but he's been working around the clock in the same style: his favorite charcoals, with accents of acrylics.

Since he's apparently not left the studio yet, I slip my feet into my flip-flops and step back out into the front yard. In the very same place where he grabbed my finger the morning after our first meeting, we've removed part of the fence and created an archway between the two.

I pause to inspect the greenhouse, which we've expanded. Happy to see that the baby Buzzes we've recently cultivated are thriving.

Archer's studio is never off-limits to me, but I enter silently anyway, in case he's in the zone and needs quiet.

While the entire home is now filled with finished pieces, in-progress pieces, and extra supplies, his favorite place to work is still his original studio. The one where we shared our first New Year's Eve kiss.

Sure enough, I find him there, on that same stool where he sat the first time I entered the space. There's one piece of charcoal tucked behind his ear and another in his fingers as he moves the stub steadily across the canvas.

Archer's gaze cuts to me as I enter the room, and though he says nothing, his gaze is warm. I brush a light kiss over his cheek so as not to disrupt his process, and smile when I see there's already a mason jar waiting for me, with the splash of Michter's that frequently marks the end of the workday and the start of *us* time.

At least until we head up to the roof, which we still do as often as weather permits, and even sometimes when it doesn't.

I'm about to take my first sip when something catches my eye.

A tiny, wrapped box beside the bottle of rye.

The scratch of Archer's charcoal never pauses as I reach for it, open it.

No diamond winks back at me. Archer knows me better.

Instead, there is a simple band. Understated, with the slightest shimmer. Made from lunar meteorite dust.

When I shift my gaze to Archer, he wordlessly pivots his easel my way so I can see what his charcoal has been working at. It's simple. Perfect. Just words.

Marry me.

Without even a second's pause, I slip the band onto my finger.

And then slide my fingers into my soon-to-be-husband's hair, pulling him in for a long, lingering kiss that leaves us both a bit breathless.

"That big 170 IQ, and you don't even want to think about it?" he asks, tucking my hair behind my ear.

"Don't need to," I say, extending my left hand to admire my new accessory. "And besides, I knew the question was coming today."

He looks genuinely nonplussed. "You did?"

"Of course." I give him a sly smile. "My horoscope told me."

Also? Archer's and my astrology charts?

The perfect match.

But you already knew that.

AUTHOR'S NOTE & ACKNOWLEDGMENTS

I've always considered myself fortunate to write fiction in my own time period, very often set in my own backyard (Manhattan).

And then . . .

I got an idea for a book about a genius physicist who wants to study astrology.

An idea that would *not* let up, no matter how much I tried to remind the muse that:

1. I am not a genius
2. I don't know much about science
3. Or astrology

Let's just say that if I were to stack up all the books I read before even starting this novel, it would be taller than a first grader.

I won't insult physicists anywhere by pretending that reading a couple of books did more than scratch the surface on the "science stuff," though I am rather proud that I can now fumble my way through a conversation about terms I didn't know existed before writing: *stellar evolution, gravitational lensing, the Hubble constant . . .*

But mostly I felt grateful that my protagonist was looking to spend an entire year *not* thinking about science, which meant I didn't have to think about it too much, either.

Astrology, on the other hand? It was at the very heart of the plot, the romance, and Miranda's character arc, and I was genuinely shocked at the complexities.

And how little I knew.

Before starting this book, here's what I knew, or thought I knew:

I was born on April 14, which makes me an Aries.

I thought we had one sign, and that signs had a couple of ideal love matches, a couple of not-so-ideal love matches.

When I conceived of this plot idea, I thought it was going to be as simple as "Miranda's a Taurus but falls for a Sagittarius. High jinks ensue."

And then . . .

My pile of astrology books arrived. (Yup, I stocked up on astrology books just like Miranda did.)

Not a single one of the books that arrived had fewer than 400 pages. The fattest among them was 801 pages.

Uh-oh.

You know that clichéd phrase "you don't know what you don't know"?

I never understood the full meaning of that sentiment until I decided to study astrology.

To say that I didn't know anything is not an understatement. Even what I thought I *did* know was wrong.

I didn't know that moon signs or ascendant signs even existed. I'd never heard the term *big three.* I didn't know you were supposed to read your horoscope based on your ascendant sign, not your sun sign. I didn't know about astrological houses.

Or house leaders.

Or Chiron.

Or planetary transits.

Or North and South Nodes.

Or aspects.

Or Saturn return.

Or progressions.

Or void-of-course moons.

Most alarmingly, considering I was setting out to write a romance, I'd never even heard the word *synastry* before, and quickly learned that my plan of pulling up a "horoscope romantic compatibility chart" wasn't only simplistic, it was outright *wrong*.

So, I read all of the books. All of them. I read some of them multiple times.

And *yet*. Even as I was familiarizing myself with all the terms, astrology still wasn't *clicking* in a way that gave me the confidence to move forward with the book.

Enter Talisa of Two Wander. My first exposure to her company was through her Traditional Astrology 101 course. I took multiple online courses, but hers was easily the most helpful. Enough so that I eventually worked up the courage to ask if I could purchase one of her natal chart readings . . . *for a fictional character.*

I emailed her with the premise of my book, and that though I'd pulled Miranda's natal chart based on her (fictional) birth details, I was struggling to understand what it all meant. I asked if she'd be willing to do the reading as though Miranda were a real person.

AUTHOR'S NOTE & ACKNOWLEDGMENTS

It's difficult to explain Talisa's unique energy that came through upon her response. But she readily agreed, exuding all things warmth and kindness. And when she delivered the PDF a couple weeks later?

It was as though the astrology fog finally lifted. All the terms I'd learned but couldn't apply, all the concepts I'd absorbed but couldn't quite grasp suddenly *clicked*. It was as though she'd delivered a personalized key to finally understanding this astrology stuff.

And when I emailed her a few weeks later, asking if I could pay her for her time to ask some questions about synastry and Miranda's ideal love match, she patiently and generously shared her knowledge without asking for anything in return.

I'm not sure anyone has ever been as instrumental in a book-writing process for me as Talisa was for *Miranda in Retrograde*. I'm not even sure the book would ever have been written if not for her!

It's impossible to explain just how kind and helpful she was, and if you're even remotely interested in astrology, I recommend starting with twowander.com. I went on to purchase my own natal chart reading from her, and it was worth every penny.

Of course, Talisa is not the only one to whom I (and *Miranda*) am indebted.

My agent, Nicole Resciniti, and my editor, Molly Gregory, were astoundingly supportive of this story from its earliest conception. Because of the unwieldiness of the plot, I needed all the support I could get, and both of these women were there every step of the way, offering encouragement and assistance without hesitation. Molly, your ability to immediately grasp what I was trying to do with this story and help me make it sparkle did not go unnoticed!

AUTHOR'S NOTE & ACKNOWLEDGMENTS

I consider myself extremely lucky to be able to work with Gallery again on this book. What they've done with the cover, the marketing, the positioning of this story has exceeded my wildest expectations. There are publishers that "put your book out there," and there are publishers who "put your book out there while tossing confetti, singing its praises, and cheering you on." Gallery is in the latter category. I'm so grateful for the entire team, from the art department, to marketing, to editorial, to production (hi, Christine!), and all of the other teams that I don't know exist but I do know I couldn't do without. Thank you!

To my husband, Anthony. Thank you. I need not explain more.

And lastly, but never least, thank *you*, reader. That you've given your valuable time to me and Miranda is a gift.

Sincerely,
Lauren
☉ Aries ☽ Taurus ↑ Cancer